Divine Christmas
Divine Cozy Mystery Series Book 5

Hope Callaghan

hopecallaghan.com
Copyright © 2019
All rights reserved.

Visit my website for new releases and special offers: hopecallaghan.com

This book is a work of fiction. Although places mentioned may be real, the characters, names and incidents, and all other details are products of the author's imagination and are fictitious. Any resemblance to actual organizations, events, or actual persons, living or dead is purely coincidental.

D1738753

i

Acknowledgments

Thank you to these wonderful ladies who help make my books shine - Peggy H., Cindi G., Jean P., Wanda D., Barbara W., Renate P. and Alix C. for taking the time to preview *Divine Christmas,* for the extra sets of eyes and for catching all of my mistakes.

A special THANKS to my reader review team:

Alice, Alta, Amary, Amy, Becky, Brenda, Carolyn, Charlene, Christine, Debbie, Denota, Devan, Diann, Grace, Helen, Jo-Ann, Jean M, Judith, Meg, Megan, Linda, Patsy, Polina, Rebecca, Rita, Theresa, Valerie and Virginia.

CONTENTS

iii

Cast of Characters

Joanna "Jo" Pepperdine. After suffering a series of heartbreaking events, Jo Pepperdine decides to open a halfway house for recently released female convicts, just outside the small town of Divine, Kansas. She assembles a small team of new friends and employees to make her dream a reality. Along the way, she comes to realize not only has she given some women a new chance at life, but she's also given herself a new lease on life.

Delta Childress. Delta is Jo's second in command. She and Jo became fast friends after Jo hired her to run the bakeshop and household. Delta is a no-nonsense asset, with a soft spot for the women who are broken, homeless, hopeless and in need of a hand up when they walk through Second Chance's doors. Although Delta isn't keen on becoming involved in the never-ending string of mysteries around town, she finds herself in over her head more often than not.

Raylene Baxter. Raylene is among the first women to come to the farm, after being released from Central State Women's Penitentiary. Raylene, a former bond agent/bounty hunter, has a knack for sleuthing out clues and helping Jo catch the bad guys.

Nash Greyson. Nash, Jo's right-hand man, is the calming force in her world of crisis. He's not necessarily on board with Jo and Delta sticking their noses into matters that are better left to the law, but often finds himself right in the thick of things, rescuing Delta and Jo when circumstances careen out of control.

Gary Stein. While Delta runs the bakeshop and household, and Nash is the all-around-handyman, Gary, a retired farmer, works his magic in Jo's vegetable gardens. A widower, he finds purpose helping Jo and the farm. Gary catches Delta's eye, and Jo wonders if there isn't a second chance...at love for Gary and Delta, too.

"And when you stand praying, if you hold anything against anyone, forgive them, so that your Father in heaven may forgive you your sins." Mark 11:25 (NIV)

Chapter 1

"Is it time yet?" Jo consulted her watch as she gazed at the others seated at the dining room table.

"I'm ready." Raylene polished off the last bite of her baked chicken.

"Me too," Kelli chimed in.

"I'll help with cleanup," Sherry offered.

"If you ladies can help Delta with the dishes, I'll get Gary and Nash to bring the Christmas tree inside and set it up."

Early that morning, Jo had cleared the perfect spot in the living room for the Christmas tree – near the front porch window and next to the fireplace.

The farm's residents scrambled out of their chairs. Everyone, other than the newest resident, Tara, who had been silent through most of dinner.

Jo wasn't the only one who noticed Tara's lack of enthusiasm in decorating the tree and hanging stockings. Nash slowly stood, giving Jo a knowing look. "Gary and I will start working on the tree stand."

"Thanks. I'll be along shortly." Jo waited until Gary and Nash headed out, the women finished clearing the table and she and Tara were alone. "You've been quiet all through dinner. Is everything all right?"

Tara slowly lifted her head; tears were streaming down her cheeks.

"Oh, dear." Jo circled around to the other side of the table and dropped down on one knee. "What's wrong?"

"I miss Keira."

Tara, who had recently been released from Central State Women's Penitentiary in Northern Kansas, was the mother of a young daughter, Keira, who was living with Tara's parents in Chicago.

Not long after arriving at the farm, Tara had confided to Jo that her parents had made it clear they wanted her to straighten out her life and be able to prove she'd changed before allowing her to have contact with the child.

Family tension was a common scenario for the former felons who arrived at the farm. The women were on probation after being released from prison and attempting to put their lives back together.

Thanksgiving, a few weeks earlier, had been difficult for the female residents. Jo was afraid Christmas, which was right around the corner, had

3

the potential to be even more of an emotional event, which was one of the reasons she was determined to create new – and happy – Christmas memories.

"You can skip the decorating if it's too upsetting."

"I...I think I will." Tara's face crumpled. She placed her hands over her eyes, her shoulders shaking as she began crying uncontrollably.

Delta appeared in the doorway, took one look at Tara's pitiful state and ran back into the kitchen. She returned, carrying a large box of tissues. "You have yourself a good cry. Jo and I are right here."

It was several long moments before the sobbing ceased. Tara lifted her head, her face splotchy and red. She hiccupped loudly. "I'm sorry."

"Ain't nothin' to be sorry about." Delta held out a handful of tissues. "We all gotta have a good cry now and then."

"Delta's right. This is a trying time of year not only for you but for the others, as well. We need to focus on moving forward, to remember all of the blessings in our lives and lean on each other when the going gets tough," Jo said wisely.

"I'm trying." Tara twisted the tissue in her hand. "I just miss my daughter and my family so much."

The women's laughter echoed from the kitchen.

She cast an anxious glance in that direction and slowly stood. "I think I'll take a pass on the decorating and go lie down."

Jo shifted back to give her room. "Would you like me to hang out with you?"

"I appreciate the offer, but I think I would rather be alone." Tara gave Jo a watery smile. "Thank you for the shoulder to cry on."

"Anytime." Jo's eyebrows knitted with concern. "Are you sure you're all right?"

"I'll be fine." Tara grabbed a few more tissues and traipsed out of the dining room.

Delta waited until the front door slammed shut. "That there is one sad woman."

Jo's shoulders slumped. "I wish I could do more to help these women. Do you think decorating and putting up a tree is a bad idea?"

"Absolutely not. What you told Tara is right. We need to focus on the good, focus on our blessings. This is the place where bad memories come to die, and happy memories are born."

Before Jo could answer, Kelli, along with the other residents, burst into the room. "We're ready."

"I think you gals set a record for kitchen cleaning," Delta teased.

Jo forced a bright smile. "Let's get busy."

"We'll start by making our stockings." Delta grabbed two big bags of craft supplies from the buffet, pulled out a stack of red velvet stockings and lined them up on the dining room table.

Kelli, the creative one of the group, followed behind Delta, placing glitter pens, fabric paint, an array of colored gemstones and embroidered snowflakes along the center.

The women began working on their handmade stockings while Jo headed to the porch to check on Nash and Gary's progress. She eased the front door open and slipped outside.

Jo shivered at the crisp evening air, rubbing the sides of her arms. "How are you doing?"

"Almost done." Gary kept a firm grip on the center of the tree while Nash slid the stand onto the base. "We had to cut off a few more of the lower branches. What do you think?"

"I think you found the perfect tree. Thank you for picking it out, Gary."

"You're welcome, Jo," Gary grinned.

"It's on." Nash wiped his hands on the front of his jeans. "We're ready to move it inside."

Jo held the door as the men carefully eased the towering pine tree through the front door. She waited for them to clear the doorway before guiding them to the spot she'd chosen. "Over here."

The men made quick work of setting the tree in front of the porch window. With a few shifts back and to the left, she deemed it the perfect location.

"Gary," Delta appeared in the doorway. "Are you ready to start on your stocking?"

"Yes, ma'am." Gary followed Delta into the dining room while Nash grabbed a lighter and ignited a small pile of newspapers inside the fireplace. "We saw Tara leave. Is everything okay?"

"She's having a hard time." Jo briefly told him about the conversation Delta and she had with the woman. "I'll check on her later."

"The holidays aren't always joyful celebrations."

"No. They're not." Jo started to say something and stopped.

"What were you going to say?"

"I was going to tell you I'm sorry your son, Ethan, won't be here for Christmas."

Nash shot Jo a quick look. "He's at an age where he thinks his friends are more important than family. Fifteen is a tricky time for teens. Thanks for giving me a few days off after the holidays to go visit him."

"You're welcome," Jo said. "Perhaps he can come and visit us in the spring. I can't wait to meet him."

"He's a good son. I only wish he lived closer."

"I'm sorry I brought it up."

"It's been in the back of my mind since he told me he wasn't coming a couple of days ago." Nash circled the tree. "What's next?"

"The lights." She reached for the strings of lights she'd placed on the coffee table. "Since you're already here, would you mind helping me put them on the tree?"

9

"Your wish is my command." Nash reached for the lights and snuck in a quick kiss.

"Hey." Jo laughed. "You're supposed to wait for the mistletoe."

"Where is it?"

"I don't have any."

Nash strode out the front door. He returned, carrying a small tree branch and dangled it over their heads. "This will have to do." He gave Jo another quick kiss.

She playfully pushed him away. "We need to get to work."

Nash began stringing the lights while Jo followed along, making sure they didn't get tangled in the branches. He had just plugged them in when the women and Gary joined them.

"The tree is beautiful," Michelle clapped her hands.

"Gary picked the perfect tree," Jo said. "And Nash did a great job with the lights. Now for the angel on top." She waited for Nash to climb onto a chair and then carefully handed him the tree topper. It was a porcelain angel, dressed in satin and lace and holding a candle in each hand.

Nash placed the angel on top and plugged her into the tree lights before hopping off. "My job here is done."

"Not yet," Jo shook her head. "We haven't made our stockings."

The women lined up in front of the fireplace, taking turns placing their stockings along the mantle while Jo and Nash hurried into the dining room to begin working on theirs.

Jo grabbed a red glitter pen and wrote her name near the top. She hot-glued several colored stones along the edge of the white fur trim and then glued a large snowflake near the bottom.

"Very creative." Nash held up an almost bare stocking. Scrawled along the top were the letters "N" and "G." What do you think of mine?"

Jo wrinkled her nose. "Where are the rest of the decorations?"

"This is it. I prefer the simple things in life."

"I can't argue the point. At least we won't have trouble figuring out which one is yours," Jo teased.

The couple returned to the living room. Jo waited for Nash to hang his stocking, and then she placed hers next to it, leaving enough room for Tara to add hers. "What's next?"

"It's time to work on stringing popcorn and making paper chains." Delta darted to the kitchen and returned juggling two large bowls of popcorn. She handed one to Sherry and the other to Kelli.

"Leah, Raylene and I will start on the paper chains," Michelle said.

"We best start hanging the ornaments." Delta placed the ornament boxes on the coffee table. As they worked, the group chatted about the upcoming holiday.

"We're finished." Kelli and Sherry started at opposite ends of the tree, carefully stringing the popcorn evenly from top to bottom.

"We're done too." Michelle stepped over the empty popcorn bowls. Leah and Raylene followed along, streaming the paper chain back and forth.

Jo watched them work. "What a great idea, Delta. I haven't made paper chains or strung popcorn since I was a kid."

"Store-bought ornaments are nice enough, but handmade decorations are the best."

They finished by hanging strands of tinsel, and then the group gathered in a semi-circle to admire their handiwork.

"This is exactly what I pictured." Jo clasped her hands, her eyes shining brightly. "It's perfect."

"It sure is," Delta nodded approvingly. "It's the prettiest tree I've ever seen."

"Time for pictures," Jo said.

There was a collective groan.

"We need to record our memories." Jo dashed to her office and grabbed her cell phone off the desk.

The first picture was a group photo, followed by a picture of each of them standing in front of the fireplace next to their stocking.

"I hate to be a party pooper, but it's getting late," Gary consulted his watch. "I need to head home."

"I'll walk you to your truck." Delta excused herself and followed him out.

"It's time for us to leave too," Michelle said. "This was a lot of fun."

The women each thanked Jo as they made their way out. Raylene was the last to leave. "Thank you, Jo, for this...for everything."

"You're welcome."

14

Raylene turned to go, and then abruptly turned back, wrapping her arms around Jo and squeezing her tight. "You're the best."

Jo blinked back sudden tears. "I...thanks."

Nash watched as Raylene released her grip and hurried out of the house. "This meant more to these women than I think you realize."

"And more to me than *they* realize."

"It is an awesome tree, and I'm not just saying that." Nash nodded toward the tree. "When's the last time you put up a Christmas tree?"

"Real or artificial?"

"Real."

"Never."

"Seriously?" Nash lifted a brow.

"The last tree I owned was metallic and silver. It was at least a decade ago."

"You haven't put up a Christmas tree in a decade?" Nash asked incredulously.

"I..." Jo lowered her gaze. "I didn't have a reason to put one up." What she didn't add is she hadn't put up a tree since her mother's death. It was too painful to think about her mother's favorite holiday. Besides, it was only Jo, and she found it easier to ignore Christmas. Her only acknowledgment of the holiday was to volunteer at the local soup kitchen serving meals to the homeless.

"I'm sorry, Jo," Nash said softly. "I'm sorry for everything you've gone through."

Jo swallowed hard, not daring to speak. Instead, she simply nodded.

"This year will be different. I promise." Nash pulled her into his arms and kissed the top of her head. "This will be the best Christmas ever."

Delta burst through the front door. She took one look at Nash and Jo embracing and slapped a hand across her eyes. "Whoa. Sorry, you two."

"Your timing is impeccable," Nash reluctantly released his grip.

"I gotta admit, I can crash the best of romantic moments."

Nash gave Jo a quick kiss and grinned at Delta. "See you in the morning."

Jo followed him to the porch and waited for him to cross the driveway. She started to close the door and then remembered Tara. "I should check on Tara before we turn in for the night."

"I'm one step ahead of you. I already did a few minutes ago," Delta said. "Her lights were off, and her door was locked."

"Then I guess I'll check on her in the morning."

"The tree looks great," Delta said.

"It's a beautiful tree."

"See you in the morning." Delta gave Jo a quick smile before making her way to the back of the house.

Jo gazed at the tree one final time before turning the lights off, a small smile on her face as she silently vowed this holiday would be a magical time for the farm's residents.

Duke, Jo's hound, led the way upstairs and to the master bedroom at the end of the hall. She made quick work of getting ready for bed before placing her prayer pillow on the floor. She clasped her hands as she knelt on top of it.

Duke waited for Jo to finish praying before leaping onto the end of the bed. She gave him a quick pat on the head before pulling the covers to her chest. "And they all settled in for a long winter's nap."

*****

The lone figure slowly inched forward, careful to avoid the overhead mercury lights that cast long shadows, leaving her exposed to whoever might be watching.

With a quick intake of breath and a furtive glance behind her, the woman crept along the back of the workshop and the barn until reaching the gardening shed.

She hugged the side of the building, not far from the thick row of bushes that separated the long stretch of empty road.

The minutes slowly ticked by as she nervously waited and watched, keeping a wary eye on the nearby buildings.

Shivering, she clutched the backpack tightly, her thin, hooded jacket doing little to ward off the night's frigid cold.

A small breeze whipped through the bushes and a blast of arctic air caught in her throat. A cough threatened to erupt. She pressed her hand to her throat. *Not now. You can't make a sound.*

Hurry. Please hurry. Where are you?

Had she missed the signal? Perhaps it was the wrong day...the wrong hour.

19

No. The timing was right.

Off in the distance, the hum of tires on the paved road grew louder. The faint beam of headlights grew brighter. The car slowed as it drew closer.

Was this it? Was this the person she was meeting?

She waited for the car to pull onto the side of the road before emerging from her hiding spot.

Whoosh. Dead leaves, caught up by a light breeze, swirled behind her. Or...was it something...someone else who was stirring the leaves?

Hurry! Run! The woman bolted across the exposed, open space, desperate to reach the vehicle, certain at any second someone would call out, would try to stop her.

The passenger side window rolled down. "Looking for a ride?" a deep husky voice asked.

"Are you going my way?"

"I am. Hop in."

For a fraction of a second, she paused, casting a frantic glance behind her. There was still time...still time to change her mind. No one would know.

It's a mistake. You're making a big mistake.

Forcing the warning voice from her mind, she climbed into the car and slammed the door shut. Moments later, the car roared off into the dark night.

*****

Jo woke early, her concern over Tara foremost in her mind. She took a quick shower and then threw on some old work clothes before she and Duke headed downstairs.

The clatter of pots and pans echoed from the kitchen. "I'm taking Duke out," Jo hollered.

Delta's head popped around the corner. "We got a frost last night. Better grab your jacket."

Jo nodded and grabbed her coat from the hook before opening the door. Duke trotted ahead, leading the way across the drive as Jo trailed behind.

Her first stop was the women's common area. Leah was the only one inside. "Is Tara around?"

"Nope." Leah shook her head. "I haven't seen her since dinner last night."

Jo thanked her and then headed to Tara's room. She rapped lightly on the door. There was no answer. She tried again and then twisted the knob. The door was unlocked.

Jo eased it open. "Tara? Are you in here?" She switched the lights on and peered into the room. A sinking feeling filled the pit of her stomach.

Chapter 2

Tara's room was surprisingly tidy, a little too tidy. Jo made a beeline for the closet. The woman's backpack, her most prized possession containing her makeup kits, was missing. The closet hangers were bare.

Jo crossed the room and yanked open the top drawer. The drawer was empty. She worked her way down the dresser, opening each of the empty drawers.

She raced out of the room and back to the common area where Leah was still inside. "Tara's room is empty. Her stuff is gone." Jo strode to the women's bathroom.

Leah trailed behind, hovering in the doorway.

"Which medicine cabinet belongs to Tara?"

"The second from the left."

Jo opened the cabinet and stared at the empty shelves. "I think Tara took off."

Leah's eyes grew wide. "She seemed sad and quiet last night during dinner."

"And you said that was the last time you saw her?"

"Yeah."

Jo eased past Leah. "I'll check the bakeshop and mercantile."

She reached the bakeshop. Raylene was standing behind the counter. "Have you seen Tara this morning?"

"No." Raylene shook her head. "Not since dinner last night."

Jo thanked her and then headed to the mercantile on the other side, where Kelli was sorting through the cash drawer, getting ready to open for business. She briefly told her what she'd found in Tara's room.

The woman's answer was the same as the others...she hadn't seen Tara since dinner the previous evening. "I think she was scheduled to work with Nash today. You might want to check with him."

"Good idea." Jo exited through the side door, making the quick trip to Nash's workshop. She gave the door a sharp rap before stepping inside.

"Hey, pretty lady."

"Hey, Nash. I'm looking for Tara. Kelli said she thought she was working with you today."

"She was scheduled to but hasn't shown up yet. I figured after last night she still wasn't feeling well."

Jo pressed a light hand to her forehead. "I think she left."

"Have you checked with Delta?"

"That's where I'm headed next." Jo returned to the house and found her friend at the kitchen table, chopping vegetables. "No one has seen Tara since dinner last night."

Michelle, who was standing at the kitchen sink, spoke. "I saw her for a few minutes after dinner. She told me she was depressed."

"Did she say anything else?" Jo asked.

"She was talking about her daughter in Chicago, how she missed her and was sad because it was the holidays. I think she was homesick."

Jo began to pace. "If we can't find her, I'll have no choice but to report her."

The women who arrived at Jo's place after being released from the Central State Women's Penitentiary, or "Central" as it was called, were on probation. Each of the resident's probation period was different, depending on the crime committed and the length of their sentence.

If Jo remembered correctly, Tara's probation was twenty-four months, and she'd only been at the farm for a couple of months. She set her mouth in a grim line. "I think we need to search the property for her."

"I'll help." Michelle wiped her hands and hurried to join Jo and Delta as they headed out.

Their first stop was the gardening shed. They found Gary inside working on his indoor greenhouse. "Uh-oh. Trouble has arrived," he teased.

"You got that right," Delta muttered. "We need your help. Tara is missing."

"Missing?" Gary peeled off his gardening gloves, a concerned look on his face.

"I want to search the grounds," Jo said. "Would you mind giving us a hand?"

"Of course not."

"Let's head to Nash's workshop to see if he can spare a few minutes to help." Jo exited the shed with the others following behind.

Nash did a double take as the group gathered inside. "No sign of Tara?"

"No one has seen her since last night. Her room is clean and empty. Her favorite backpack is missing."

"She took her backpack everywhere she went," Nash said. "I guess the first thing we need to do is search the farm."

"I was thinking the same thing." Jo split the group up. Gary would start his search in the gardens. Nash offered to search the outbuildings. Delta was in charge of searching the main house.

"I have a set of master keys. Michelle and I will search the residents' units and common areas," Jo said. "I need to stop by the mercantile and bakeshop to let the women know I'm checking their units."

Michelle waited on the porch while Jo made her way inside the mercantile.

"No sign of Tara?" Kelli asked.

"No. I need to search all of the units and wanted to give you a heads up."

"No problem," Kelli said. "Good luck."

Jo crossed over to the bakeshop and waited until Raylene finished helping a customer. "There's no sign of Tara. I need to search all of the units."

"Fine by me." Raylene shook her head. "If she took off, that was a dumb move. Do you need me to let you in?"

Jo jangled the set of master keys. "It's not necessary. I just wanted to give you a heads up."

"No problem. Don't mind the mess."

"That's the least of my worries." Since Sherry was already working her morning shift at Marlee's deli, Jo gave her a quick call. After a brief explanation about Tara's disappearance, Sherry gave her the green light to search her room. "I hope you find her."

"I hope so too." Jo ended the call and joined Michelle.

The women searched the first three units, working their way to the common area, which separated the second set of units. Jo inspected the contents of each of the bathroom's medicine cabinets before returning to the living room where Michelle was sorting through the living room's desk cubbies.

Jo motioned to the laptops nearby. "Did Tara ever use the laptops?"

"Yeah," Michelle nodded. "We all use them. In fact, I'm pretty sure she was using one before dinner last night."

Jo stepped closer. "Which one?"

"Let me think." Michelle scratched her chin. "I'm almost certain it was the one on the end."

Jo eased into an empty chair and turned the computer on. She waited for the login screen to pop up and entered the password used by the residents. An empty search screen appeared. Jo clicked on the down arrow, revealing a field of recent searches.

One was makeup tips. Another was the greyhound bus schedule, and the third, the one that caused Jo's stomach to somersault, was a search on violating probation.

Michelle, who was standing directly behind Jo, let out a small gasp. "She took off."

"It appears to be the case," Jo said grimly. "If what you said was true, she may be on her way to Chicago. It will be a long trip from here to Illinois, even if she manages to make it to the nearest bus station."

"You have to report her."

"She's left me no choice." Jo finished scrolling through the rest of the recent searches, clicked out of the screen and logged off. "We might as well search the other three units."

It didn't take long for Jo and Michelle to finish inspecting the other units. "Let's head back to the workshop."

The workshop was empty when they arrived. Delta joined them moments later. "The house is clean, but then Tara never wandered around inside, even when she was helping me in the kitchen. How about you? Any luck?"

"Yeah. I'll wait until Gary and Nash return to tell you what we found."

"It's not good," Delta guessed.

"Nope."

It was another fifteen minutes before Nash joined them. Gary was the last to arrive. "I'm sorry it took me so long. There's a lot of ground to cover."

"Thanks for helping with the search," Jo said gratefully. "Michelle and I found something on one of the residents' computers." She explained how Tara had searched bus schedules and consequences for violating probation.

"Then she left voluntarily," Delta said. "She's gonna be in a heap of trouble."

"Yes, she will. I might as well call her probation officer."

"Before you do, I think I may have found another clue." Nash handed Jo a plastic bag. "I found this in the workshop's trashcan."

Chapter 3

"What is it?" Jo asked.

"It's a store receipt."

She studied the small slip of paper, a receipt for a Tracfone, a contraband item since none of the residents were allowed to have personal cell phones. Instead, they borrowed the house phone or used Jo's cell phone if they needed to make a call.

"Someone at the farm bought a phone." Jo waved the receipt in the air. "Anyone here recently purchase a phone?"

Nash, Delta, Gary and Michelle shook their heads.

"It could've been one of the other women," Nash said.

"I'll be right back." Jo trekked back to the bakeshop, where Raylene was arranging cream cheese cupcakes on an empty display tray. She handed her the receipt. "Do you know anything about this?"

Raylene's eyes squinted as she studied the receipt. "No. This is for a cell phone. Where did you find it?"

"Nash found it in the workshop's trashcan."

"It's not mine."

"I didn't think so." Jo crossed over into the mercantile. Kelli, who was behind the counter, watched Jo approach. "Still no sign of Tara?"

"No. Nash found this in the workshop trashcan."

Kelli glanced at the receipt and shook her head. "I've never seen this before. This is a contraband item. I would be crazy to buy one and try to hide it from you."

"Yes, it is, and yes, you would be." Jo thanked her before returning to the shop where the others were waiting.

"Well?" Delta asked. "Anyone own up to buying the phone?"

"No." Jo inspected the receipt closely. "This receipt is from the superstore in Centerpoint." She shifted her gaze to Delta. "What day did Tara and I go shopping in Centerpoint?"

"Two days ago. It was Tuesday. I remember the day because I asked you to pick up some fresh ground beef for our Taco Tuesday's dinner."

"It's the same day this Tracfone was purchased at the store where Tara and I shopped. She must've somehow managed to buy this without my knowledge."

"Which means she could easily have arranged for someone to pick her up last night," Delta said. "Now what?"

"I'm going to have to call her probation officer."
Jo trudged back to the house and into her office.
She placed the receipt on the desk before unlocking
the filing cabinet. Jo pulled Tara's progress file from
the drawer and flipped it open.

Looking back, the signs were all there. Jo had
suspected all along Tara wasn't happy at the farm
and had been keeping an eye on her, but apparently
not close enough.

Jo blew air through thinned lips and dialed Ed
Shevock's, Tara's probation officer, number. She left
a brief message, and after ending the call, she stared
out the window, wondering how long Tara had been
planning to leave.

The woman had to know she would eventually be
caught and returned to prison to finish her
sentence. Was she that desperate to return to
Chicago for a brief visit to see her daughter?

From what Jo gathered from snippets of her
conversations with Tara, the few times the woman

had called her family to check on her daughter, she'd been met with a chilly reception.

Perhaps the pull was so strong Tara was willing to risk her freedom for a chance to spend fleeting moments with her child.

It was an emotion Jo was certain only a parent could understand. She was all too familiar with the hollow, empty feeling she'd worked through for years after her parents' deaths.

At the bottom of Tara's notes, Jo had written "50/50" and remembered thinking her newest resident had a fifty-fifty chance of making it through the next two years at the farm.

She returned the folder to the drawer, leaned back in the chair and closed her eyes, which is where Delta found her a short time later.

"I take it the call to Tara's probation officer didn't go well." Delta didn't wait for an invitation and plopped down in an empty chair.

"I left a message. I'm still waiting for a call back." Jo lifted her head. "Would you have done it? Run away, I mean, to see your child?"

"I don't know. I can't say for certain," Delta shrugged. "I would hope I would think far enough ahead to know a couple of years in the scheme of things isn't a long time. She should've sucked it up and stayed put."

"It would've been the wise thing to do. I was sitting here thinking about therapists."

"After all you've been through, I'm surprised you don't have one on speed dial," Delta joked.

"Right?" Jo smiled. "I meant for the women. All of them have been through a lot. Do you think if Tara had been able to talk to a professional, she might not have taken off?"

"I honestly don't know. It's something to think about."

Jo's cell phone chimed, and she glanced at the screen. "It's Tara's probation officer calling me back." She pressed the answer button. "Joanna Pepperdine speaking."

"This is Officer Ed Shevock returning your call."

"Thank you for calling me back. Tara Cloyne has gone missing," Jo blurted out. "We've searched the entire property. There's no sign of her. Her belongings are missing, and we believe she may have a Tracfone with her."

"How long has she been missing?"

"No one has seen her since last night. She may be headed to Chicago to see her daughter."

The officer asked Jo several more questions. He thanked her for the heads up and promised to call her back if, or when, he found anything. Jo promised the same before ending the call and tossing the phone on top of the desk. "That call pretty much sealed her fate."

"Tara sealed her fate the moment she decided to run off." Delta scooched out of the chair. "The reason I'm here is Marlee is looking for you.

Something about Pastor Murphy asking for an emergency DABO meeting over at the deli at eleven."

"A meeting?" Jo let out a small sigh.

DABO, short for Divine Area Business Owners, was a group of locals who met once a month to discuss promoting the area businesses, issues of concern and upcoming events.

Marlee, the owner of Divine Delicatessen and Jo's friend, had recently convinced her to join the group. At first, Jo resisted. She had plenty on her plate to keep her busy between managing Second Chance Mercantile and Divine Baked Goods shop, not to mention overseeing the women who lived at the farm.

"How in the world did I ever let Marlee talk me into joining that group?"

"Because you're a successful area businesswoman. It's your duty to keep up on the business happenings and contribute to the success of Divine."

"I suppose. I guess that means I better get going." Jo left a message for Marlee, letting her know she was on her way and then followed Delta into the kitchen. She snatched her keys off the hook. "Hopefully, this won't take long."

It was a short drive from the farm to the small town of Divine. The parking spots in front of the deli were all full, forcing Jo to park at the other end of the street, not far from Claire's Collectibles & Antique Shop.

She sprang from the vehicle and onto the sidewalk as Claire, another of Jo's friends, stepped out of her store. "Hey, Jo."

"Hi, Claire. You heading to the DABO meeting?"

"I am. I wonder what's going on. This is the first time in a long time someone called an emergency meeting."

"From what Marlee told Delta, it has something to do with Pastor Murphy."

The women reached the front of the deli, and Claire slowed. "Great. He's here."

"He who?"

"Harrison Cantwell. He owns half the town and is the area's number one landlord. He's also a rude and ruthless jerk."

"How come I've never heard the name before?"

"Because you're lucky? His family's been in Divine for as long as I can remember. At one time, they owned hundreds of acres of farmland. After Harrison's parents died, he started selling off the land and buying up vacant properties. In fact, he owns the old movie theater your half-brother, Miles, is interested in purchasing. Speaking of Miles, how's that going?"

Some months back, Miles Parker had shown up on Jo's doorstep, claiming his mother and Jo's father, Andrew Carlton, had an affair and that he was her half-brother. At first, Jo refused to believe it, but DNA tests revealed he was telling the truth.

She was still reeling from the shocking news when Miles's attorney drafted a tentative agreement, seeking half of what her parents had left her.

"We're at a standstill. His attorney and my attorney have gone back and forth for weeks now, trying to hammer out an agreement. My attorney was finally able to convince Miles to agree to a more reasonable settlement. The major sticking point now is that he's adamant about staying in the area."

"It sounds like a mess."

"It is," Jo sighed heavily. "We'll be lucky to reach an agreement by New Year's."

Jo recognized a few familiar faces as she and Claire zigzagged toward an empty table in the back, next to Wayne and Charlotte Malton, the owners of Tool Time Hardware.

Sherry joined them and began filling Jo's coffee cup. "Hey, Jo. Claire."

"Hi, Sherry. How's it going?"

"Busy. Not that I'm complaining. Busy means more tips."

Marlee, who stood near the front, began waving her hands. "Let's get this meeting started. Without further ado, I'll let Pastor Murphy take over." She motioned to the pastor, who stood off to the side.

"Thank you, Marlee, and thank you, everyone, for coming here on such short notice," Pastor Murphy said. "Something terrible has happened, and I need your help."

Chapter 4

"As many of you know, each year Divine Church of God sponsors Spirit of the Season," Pastor Murphy said. "We purchase toys and Christmas gifts for children in our community who would otherwise go without."

Jo was familiar with the pastor's outreach. She had already donated to the worthwhile cause in memory of her mother. She also planned to make a contribution from her business but hadn't gotten around to it yet.

"For those of you not familiar with Spirit of the Season, parents, neighbors, area teachers, family and friends are given the opportunity to submit a child's name, starting with newborns all the way to the age of seventeen. This season we have a record number of children who are signed up for the program."

The pastor continued. "We already purchased roughly ninety percent of the gifts, which were being kept in the church's storage building. Unfortunately, someone broke in and stole everything two nights ago."

Jo's jaw dropped.

"Oh no," Claire mumbled.

"All of the gifts are gone."

"You mean someone had the nerve to steal children's Christmas presents?" Wayne Malton shook his head.

"Every last gift, down to coloring books and crayons," the pastor said grimly. "It appears we have a Scrooge in our midst."

"What are you going to do?" Jo asked.

The pastor shrugged helplessly. "I'm doing the only thing I can think of, and that's to ask you for help in replacing the toys and gifts. Anything you're able to give at this point would be nothing short of a Christmas miracle."

"I'll help," Marlee said.

"Me too," Claire chimed in.

"This is ridiculous," Harrison Cantwell huffed. "If you can't afford to take care of children, then don't have them. Life is full of tough breaks. Better for the kids to learn early on what it's like to go without than to go through life expecting handouts."

"Harrison," Marlee chided. "What a terrible thing to say."

"Talk about a Scrooge," Wayne Malton said.

Harrison glared at Wayne. "You're late with your rent payment, so if I were you, I'd would keep my mouth shut."

Chief Tallgrass, from the nearby Indian reservation, spoke. "We will donate again. You are doing a good thing, pastor."

"Before we get all wishy-washy with good cheer and you people start parting with your hard-earned money, I have some real business to discuss." Harrison abruptly stood. "I want to discuss a business application for my movie theater."

Marlee narrowed her eyes. "The theater has been closed for almost a decade. What are your plans?"

"I'm selling it. The potential purchaser would like to turn it into a combination movie and dinner theater."

"Another eating establishment."

"Yep." Cantwell nodded. "Got a solid buyer lined up who's waiting for the financing to come through. The deal is contingent on me getting a variance so he can open the place as a package deal." The man droned on about expanding Divine's community presence, bringing new people to the area and re-investing tax money into the downtown area.

"Only if it benefits him," Claire whispered under her breath.

"We'll put it on the schedule for next month's meeting. In the meantime, we'll need more information and details about the proposed project," Marlee said.

"This is ridiculous," Harrison grunted. "Nothing in this group moves forward in a timely manner. DABO is a total waste of time. I might as well quit the group."

"Good riddance," Claire muttered.

Harrison shot her a hard look. "You need to clean up your alley before I file a complaint with the county."

"You're a jerk," Claire shot back.

Harrison ignored the comment as he zeroed in on Jo. "Who are you?" he asked rudely.

Jo lifted her chin and met his gaze. "I'm Joanna Pepperdine. I own Second Chance Mercantile and Divine Baked Goods Shop."

"Uh." Harrison made a grunting noise. "You're the goody two shoes who is housing a bunch of criminals."

"The women who reside at the farm have paid their dues," she replied in a tight voice. "They're working hard to lead productive, meaningful lives and learning new skills to move them forward."

Harrison Cantwell smirked. "They ought to try a little harder."

"What's that supposed to mean?"

"I've been by your bakeshop. On my last visit, one of the employees reached into the display case without wearing gloves. I immediately reported it to the local health department."

The blood drained from Jo's face. "An employee wasn't wearing gloves and touched the food?"

"She used a pair of plastic tongs instead, violating food safety codes."

"You, sir, are a troublemaker." Jo jabbed a finger in his direction. "My businesses are regularly inspected. I can assure you I haven't been cited for a single violation."

"Until now." Harrison's face contorted. "Businesses get sued for causing food poisoning."

"Are you saying goods from my bakeshop made you sick?" Jo was horrified someone would suggest such a thing.

"You'll find out soon enough."

Jo bit back a scathing reply, wondering what had happened in Harrison Cantwell's life to make him such an angry and bitter old man. "And you have no proof," she said coolly. "We'll be sure to pray for you at the dinner table this evening."

"I don't need anybody talkin' to God about me."

There was a commotion near the entrance, and Carrie Ford, another Divine local, rushed inside. "I'm sorry that I'm late." Perched on her shoulder was a small black object, its beak bobbing up and down as she scurried to the back. She cast Jo and Claire an apologetic smile on her way past.

"Carrie. I forgot you were stopping by." Marlee addressed the group. "Carrie asked that she be allowed to speak to DABO regarding her home-based business."

"Is that a bird?" Jo leaned in.

"I...it looks like it," Claire whispered under her breath.

Carrie had almost reached the front when she tripped on the leg of Wayne Malton's chair. She stumbled forward, throwing her hands out in front of her to break her fall.

Wayne sprang into action, catching Carrie on her way down. The sudden move dislodged the critter from its perch atop her shoulder, smacking him in the face before hitting the floor.

He helped steady her and gingerly touched the peck mark on the side of his cheek.

"I...I'm so sorry, Wayne." Carrie snatched the creature off the floor, placing it back on her shoulder before joining Marlee.

"Make it quick," Cantwell said loudly. "What's that black mess on your shoulder?"

"This is Myron." Carrie reached up and patted his head. "Myron is the mascot for Carrie's Custom Creations."

"You have a dead bird strapped to your shoulder." Cantwell burst out laughing. "Maybe this isn't such a waste of time after all."

Marlee motioned for him to be quiet. "Continue Carrie."

"I've taken over my deceased husband's taxidermy business. I'm in the process of rebranding it so I can reach more customers." Carrie explained she was hoping the Divine area business owners could help her spread the word and increase her presence in the community. "Now that the fall hunting season is over, business has dropped off, so I came up with an ingenious way to reach new customers."

"I'll let Myron tell you." Carrie gently extracted Myron from her shoulder and ran a light hand over his tufted chest.

"Carrie's Custom Creations. Vault the voices of your loved ones for a small monthly fee."

Jo strained to hear. "What did Myron say?"

"Maybe I didn't record it loud enough." Carrie pressed on his chest and he repeated the phrase.

"Vault the voices of your loved ones," Wayne Malton said.

"Yes." Carrie nodded eagerly. "Isn't it brilliant? Clients will be able to send me expressions of love from family members. I'll store them for future use. When their loved one passes, their voice can be added to the precious creation of their choice. They'll be with them forever."

"You mean to say your business plan is to have customers record the voices of someone who is ready to kick the bucket and then they send it to you for safekeeping?" Cantwell rolled his eyes. "You should rename your business Crazy Carrie's Creepy Creations."

"Harrison," Marlee shook her head. "That's enough."

Carrie waved dismissively. "Harrison can say whatever he likes. We all know who the real crazy creep around here is."

"What's that supposed to mean?"

"You know exactly what I'm talking about."

"This is nonsense." He stormed to the front of the restaurant, flung the door open and marched out.

"Carrie managed to ruffle Harrison's feathers." Claire grinned as she motioned to Myron. "No pun intended."

"I say good riddance," Wayne Malton grunted.

"Can't we run the rotten man out of town?" his wife joked.

"I wish," Marlee sighed.

"At the risk of sounding like Debbie Downer, I'm going to add my two cents and admit a deceased person's voice inside a dead animal strikes me as a tad bit morbid," Claire wrinkled her nose.

"Morbid?" Carrie shook her head. "I think it's a brilliant idea. What I wouldn't give to be able to hear my husband's voice again."

"Abner?" Marlee asked.

"No. George, husband number three."

"It's an interesting business plan," Jo said diplomatically. "How can we help?"

"I printed some flyers." Carrie carefully placed Myron back on her shoulder before reaching into her purse and pulling out a small stack of papers. "I was hoping those of you with retail businesses...actually all of you here with the exception of Harrison, could help me by posting flyers on your boards or leaving them next to your cash registers."

"I'll post them in the bakeshop and mercantile," Jo said.

"Thanks, Jo." Carrie handed her a couple of flyers.

"I'll take one for the laundromat and another for my antique shop." Claire held out her hand.

"We will." Wayne Malton made his way over and took some sheets from Carrie.

"I've already told you I'll post them on the bulletin board," Marlee said.

Pastor Murphy, who had remained silent during Carrie's speech and the heated words between Harrison Cantwell and the woman, stepped forward. "I'll take one too and post it on the church's bulletin board."

"Thank you, everyone," Carrie beamed. "I appreciate your help. As a token of my appreciation, I'm offering each of you twenty-five percent off your first order."

"That's...very kind." Claire smiled.

"You sure managed to get under Cantwell's skin," Wayne remarked.

"He knows better than to mess with me." Carrie handed out the last flyer.

"And now that we've finished our official business, the meeting is adjourned," Marlee said. "For those of you who are in a position to contribute to Pastor Murphy's emergency needs, I know I speak for him when I tell you it would be greatly appreciated."

Jo hung back and watched as Claire and the area business owners gathered around the pastor, her heart swelling with pride.

The restaurant's dining room eventually cleared. Marlee returned to the kitchen, leaving Jo and Pastor Murphy alone.

"Hello, Jo," Pastor Murphy gave her a sad smile. "Can you spare an extra dime for the kids?"

"I can spare more than a dime." Jo nodded toward the handful of checks the pastor was holding. "Divine is a wonderful place, full of caring people. At the risk of sounding nosy, how much have you collected to replace what you lost?"

"Three hundred dollars."

"And how much more do you need?"

"Probably another seven...seven hundred."

"I'll make up the difference. Second Chance will, but only if you agree to one thing."

It took a second for Jo's generous offer to sink in, and the pastor's eyes filled with tears. "I can't let you..."

Jo lifted a hand. "I insist."

"I don't know what to say."

"You haven't heard my bargain," she teased.

"It doesn't matter. Whatever you want, it's yours."

"I want to host Spirit of the Season at the farm. I want to turn Nash's workshop into Santa's workshop, complete with Santa, Mrs. Claus and a band of merry elves."

"Are you serious?" The pastor's eyes grew wide.

Jo quickly warmed to the idea. "Yes. In fact, if you can get the children over to the farm on the day you planned to distribute the gifts, I'll have everything ready to go for a Winter Wonderland, a visit from Santa, cookies, milk. Shoot, I may even be able to round up a reindeer or two."

"We can use the church bus to bring them to you. I'm at a loss." The pastor's lower lip trembled. "God has surely dropped an angel right on our doorstep."

"You're being too kind." Jo reached into her purse, pulled out her checkbook and a pen. She wrote a check for eight hundred dollars and handed it to him.

He glanced at the amount, and she thought he was going to pass out. "Jo..."

Jo quickly cut him off. "We'll follow up on the details, but it looks as if I'm going to have to get busy creating a magical Christmas party. This will be good for the women and good for me."

The pastor impulsively grabbed Jo and hugged her tight. "I think I love you."

She burst out laughing. "I love you too."

"I...I better get going. I have a lot of shopping to do."

"After you buy the gifts, drop them off at the farm, and I'll have Santa's elves start wrapping them. We have plenty of room to store the presents in my barn."

"I can't tell you how much this means to me, what it will mean to the children." The pastor squeezed Jo's hand. "God bless you."

Jo watched as he strolled out of the restaurant, a spring in his step.

Sherry, who had wandered over and caught the tail end of the conversation, spoke. "I thought he was gonna hit the floor."

"I thought so too," Jo chuckled.

"I'm guessing I'll be one of the merry elves."

"Do you mind?"

"Are you kidding?" Sherry grinned. "I can't wait. This is going to be awesome."

"I hope the others will think so too."

"They will," Sherry motioned to the door. "What do you think about that jerk, Harrison Cantwell?"

"I hope God grabs hold of the man's heart."

"Any news on Tara?"

"No." Jo's expression sobered. "She's gone. I suspect she's on her way to Chicago to see her daughter."

"She made a huge mistake," Sherry said.

"I'm afraid she has." Jo stopped by the back to thank Marlee for hosting the meeting and then headed out.

On the drive home, Jo began mentally planning for the Christmas party. As she pulled into the drive, she noticed a strange vehicle in her rearview mirror following close behind. They followed her into the driveway and parked near the front porch.

Jo eased into her parking spot, grabbed her purse and climbed out.

The vehicle's occupant exited the car, and Jo's heart plummeted when she recognized the driver.

Chapter 5

"Hello, Joanna." Miles Parker offered Jo a hesitant smile.

"Hello," she replied in an even tone. "I didn't recognize your car."

"I turned in the rental and purchased a vehicle since it appears I'll be in the area indefinitely."

"You can leave anytime. No one is stopping you," Jo said coolly.

"Ah, but that's not true. We still have the matter of a signed settlement agreement."

"Which can be signed anywhere in the world. There's no reason for you to stay in Divine."

Miles shoved his hands in his pockets and gazed around. "Divine is a nice area. This place is growing on me. I'm learning to appreciate the friendliness and strong sense of community of a small town. Not to mention that the cost of living here is reasonable, unlike California."

"What's the real reason you won't leave?" Jo asked bluntly.

"I just told you."

"And I don't believe it. I think you're here because of me."

Miles opened his mouth to say something. An unreadable expression crossed his face, and Jo almost thought he looked sad.

"You're right. I'm still here because of you."

Jo stared him down until Miles looked away. "This is my home."

"It is, and from what the locals tell me, you've managed to win most of them over." Miles nodded toward the women's units in the back. "Not everyone can successfully house a group of former prison inmates, reintroduce them to society and be accepted by the community."

"These women are working hard to straighten out their lives. The residents of Divine have welcomed us graciously and warmly. I believe God has a special blessing for people who are willing to give others another chance."

"See, that's it."

"What's it?"

Miles rubbed a light hand across his brow, and the fleeting look Jo had glimpsed earlier returned. "I'm here to apologize. For the way I blew into town, showed up on your doorstep and dropped the bomb about our father. I was hurt. I was angry. Put yourself in my shoes for one second." He paused, staring earnestly at Jo, as if begging her to see his side of things.

The fact of the matter was Jo had tried to put herself in Miles's shoes. Her father was no saint. In fact, far from it. Looking back, she shouldn't have been shocked that her father, who carried on extramarital affairs for years, had fathered a son.

What did surprise her was how he had convinced Miles's mother to move across the country, to California, and had managed to pay her off secretly for years...decades even.

The realization her father led a double life made Jo wonder if she had even more half-siblings running around, ones she hadn't yet met.

Who wouldn't be hurt to find out their father had no interest in being a part of their lives, and not even knowing who that person was until their mother died and they uncovered the shocking truth? That Andrew Carlton, a wealthy businessman from Kansas, worth millions, had left his entire estate to Jo, his only known heir?

She couldn't fault him on any of those fronts. "I understand how the discovery of who your father was could fill you with rage, but you must also put yourself in my shoes, to have a complete stranger show up claiming to be related."

"Agreed." Miles paused, as if choosing his next words carefully. "Like you, except for a distant aunt, I have no other family. I was an only child."

Miles lifted his gaze, and their eyes met, an almost apologetic, pleading look in his, but also questioning as if he was waiting for her to give him some sort of answer.

Jo had spent years working on forgiveness...forgiving her father, forgiving the people responsible for putting her mother behind bars and mostly forgiving herself. Could she find it in her heart to forgive again?

The front porch's screen door banged shut. She didn't look, but Jo knew it was Delta checking on her. "I appreciate you coming here to apologize. I'm sure it took a lot for you to do that, but I'm not going to change my mind about the terms of the agreement."

"I see." Miles glanced over Jo's shoulder. "Thank you for not kicking me off your property without hearing me out." He slowly climbed into his car and pulled out of the driveway. Jo watched until the car turned onto the road and disappeared.

Delta made her way down the steps. "I wouldn't have believed Miles Parker was in our driveway had I not seen it with my own two eyes. What was that all about?"

"He said he wanted to apologize."

"And you believe him?"

"No. Maybe. I don't know," Jo confessed. "He seemed sincere."

Delta cleared her throat. "Well, we should never be holding a grudge, especially when we never know when our time is up, and we're about to face our maker."

"Well said."

"How was the meeting?"

Jo briefly filled Delta in on Pastor Murphy's situation. "What do you think about turning this place into Santa's workshop?"

"It's a grand idea. Who will be Santa?"

"I was thinking Gary." Jo paused. "And I have the perfect Mrs. Claus in mind."

"Me?"

"Yes, you. Well?"

"I reckon I got the figure for it." Delta patted her ample hips.

"Perfect. Now all I have to do is sweet talk Nash into building a sleigh large enough to hold Jolly Old Saint Nick."

"You got that man wrapped around your little finger." Delta linked her arm with Jo's, and they meandered up the steps.

"I met Harrison Cantwell."

"That old curmudgeon is still around? I thought he kicked the bucket years ago."

"He's very much alive and not a nice person. He made some uncalled-for comments about the farm and its residents. I blew my cool and gave him a

71

piece of my mind before telling him I would pray for him."

"Harrison can get under the skin of a saint. Don't pay him no mind. I think he joined DABO because he's nosy and likes to irritate everyone."

"He's doing an excellent job." Jo changed the subject. "You still on for taking Curtis to the vet tomorrow?"

"Yes. Yes, I am. He's not gonna like it."

"I imagine that's true, which is why we're going to tag-team it. One of us keeps him corralled while the other drives."

The rest of the afternoon passed uneventfully with Jo spending time in her office going over the rest of the residents' sheets, Tara still first and foremost in the back of her mind.

Delta stopped by late afternoon to ask about dinner.

"It's been a busy day. Why not give yourself a break and order pizza?"

"You sure? I feel like I'm shirking my duties."

Jo waved dismissively. "I think pizza would be perfect."

Delta promised to order several pies for delivery around six while Jo finished her file updates before returning to her email inbox. At the top of the inbox was a copy of the most recent agreement from Miles and his attorney.

Her eyes were drawn to the dollar amount – two million dollars. It was an amount that took Jo's breath away but was still less than what had been originally requested. The only sticking point now was Miles's insistence he be allowed to reside wherever he wanted, including Divine.

Jo thought about their conversation and his apology. He struck her as being genuine, even sad. What if Miles was repentant about what he'd said to her? What if all he was looking for was family?

73

Wasn't it the same thing she craved? She had worked hard to create her own family...the farm's residents, Nash, Gary and Delta. The Bible verse about forgiving others ran through her head:

"And when you stand praying, if you hold anything against anyone, forgive them, so that your Father in heaven may forgive you your sins." Mark 11:25 (NIV)

God could not forgive her if she didn't forgive Miles. And if she was completely honest with herself, there was a small part of her that understood his actions. What Jo's father had done was despicable, not only to Jo and her mother but also to Miles and his mother.

Jo had long ago forgiven her father for his indiscretions. She no longer blamed him for her mother's actions and his tragic death. And that was all it was...a tragic set of events put in motion with an outcome that ruined lives.

She exited the screen. Miles had extended the olive branch. It was up to her to decide if she wanted to accept it. Her heart told her she needed to. Deciding to sleep on it, Jo wandered into the kitchen.

Delta was seated at the table. Gary sat next to her, their heads close together. Nash was on the other side.

"You're having a meeting, and I wasn't invited?" Jo joked.

"We're going over tentative plans for the children's visit to Santa's workshop. I got so excited when Gary and Nash stopped by to ask about the business meeting, I spilled the beans."

"That's okay." Jo pulled out a chair. "It will be an awesome way to create a special memory for the kids. I mean, what child wouldn't love a visit with Santa Claus?"

The group discussed the first step...Nash's construction of a sleigh large enough for Gary a/k/a Santa.

"Pastor Murphy should be dropping off the first load of gifts sometime tomorrow. I hope I'm not pushing it, but the Spirit of the Season date for giving the gifts is next Saturday."

"I think we can swing it if we get started on it right away," Nash said confidently. "I'll have to push all of my other projects aside."

"I can help," Gary offered. "The gardens are done for the season, so I have some free time."

"Perfect," Jo beamed. "It looks as if Santa's workshop and the children's visit is a go."

Delta grabbed a yellow pad and started taking notes. "We'll need a Santa suit and a Mrs. Claus outfit."

"And six elves' costumes," Jo said.

"Right." Delta stopped scribbling. "What about you?"

"I'll be working behind the scenes."

"Gary and I will start working on the sleigh and the reindeer first thing tomorrow morning," Nash said.

The front bell rang, and Jo slid out of her chair. "The pizza is here. The women should be heading over any time now."

Instead of gathering around the dining room table, Jo and Delta decided on a serve-yourself casual meal in the living room where they could admire the Christmas tree.

Jo waited for everyone to grab a plate of food and join her in the living room before filling the female residents in on her plans to host a Santa's workshop for the area children.

"Who is Santa?" Raylene asked.

Jo jabbed her finger in Gary's direction. "Gary will be Jolly Old Saint Nick. Delta is going to be Mrs. Claus. I do need a few elves to help Santa." Her eyes traveled around the room. "Anyone care to volunteer?"

"I will," the women answered in unison.

"How fun," Michelle clapped her hands. "Will we get to wear elf costumes?"

"Yes. As a matter of fact, I found a couple of strong contenders during an online search." Jo darted to her office, grabbed the sheets she'd printed off and returned to the living room where she passed them around. "Majority rules. I'll let you decide among yourselves."

The women gathered in a circle. They quickly and unanimously picked out an elf costume. Jo promised she would be ordering them first thing in the morning, along with Santa and Mrs. Claus outfits.

Delta finished her last bite of pizza and grabbed a napkin. "First, we gotta get some measurements."

With Jo's assistance, Delta took the women's measurements while Nash jotted them down on the back of the paper of their chosen elf costume. Gary's measurements were next and then Delta, who insisted Mrs. Claus needed to match Santa.

"While you finish up, we'll take care of the leftovers and plates." Raylene picked up the empty pizza boxes while Kelli, Michelle and Leah gathered the dirty dishes.

Raylene was the first to return to the living room. "Any word on Tara?"

"No." Jo somberly shook her head. "Not a peep. I spoke with her probation officer. If, or should I say when, they find her, she'll be heading back to Central."

"I better get going. I'm working an early shift at the restaurant in the morning," Sherry said.

Marlee's really bumped up your hours." Jo followed her to the front door.

"Yeah. The deli is hosting a bunch of Christmas luncheons." Sherry looked as if she were going to say something else.

"What is it?"

Sherry shot the others a quick look, and Jo nodded knowingly. "We'll chat after everyone is gone."

They stood off to the side, waiting for the other residents to leave. Delta and Gary were next. Nash lingered in the doorway, giving Jo's hand a gentle squeeze. "See you tomorrow?"

"Yes. Bright and early to make sure we clear out enough room for the children's Christmas presents." Jo closed the door behind him and turned to Sherry. "Let's have a seat."

Sherry followed her into the living room and perched on the edge of the couch.

"Is everything all right?"

"I overheard something after the business meeting and thought you should know. It was the old man, the one who was ranting about giving money for the children's gifts."

"Harrison Cantwell," Jo said.

"Yes. I think that was his name. He came back to the deli and sat in the corner. Another man came in. They were talking in low voices. I heard them mention Marlee and the nice couple who own the hardware store."

"The Maltons."

"The Maltons," Sherry repeated. "He mentioned your name too. He must not have known I was a resident here. He said something about an investigation."

Jo's heart skipped a beat. "An investigation?"

Sherry nodded. "I'm not sure if it had to do with you. I tried to act like I wasn't listening. When I went back to check on them, they looked like they were arguing. The man left, and Mr. Cantwell left a short time later."

"Thank you for the heads up." Jo patted Sherry's arm. "From what I've been told, Mr. Cantwell likes to cause trouble around town. I appreciate you letting me know, but don't worry about it."

There was a look of relief on Sherry's face. "I hope it was nothing. I better get going."

After Sherry left, Jo let Duke out for a final potty break and patrol, passing Delta, who was on her way in.

The night air was chilly, and the pup made quick work of taking care of business before bolting back inside. Jo trailed behind, following him into the kitchen.

The light over the stove was on. Delta was nowhere in sight. She could hear her television blaring loudly in the bedroom.

Jo tiptoed up the stairs and quickly slipped into her pajamas. While brushing her teeth, she thought about Tara and hoped that wherever she was – she was safe.

Once in bed, she quickly fell asleep but woke halfway through the night and began tossing and turning. Finally, in the early hours of the morning, Jo gave up on sleep and stumbled downstairs to start a pot of coffee.

Delta was already up. "You look rough."

"I'm worried about Tara. I'm wondering if I'm in over my head with Santa's workshop since it's such short notice." Jo poured a cup of coffee and slumped into a chair. "Sherry said she overheard Harrison Cantwell mention my name and an investigation while talking with another man at Marlee's place after our meeting yesterday."

"The man is nothing but trouble." Delta set a plate of donuts on the table and sank into the chair next to her friend. "I bet he's got the county sheriff on speed dial and probably the state police, too."

Jo sipped her coffee, eyeing her friend over the rim. "What do you think about Miles's apology?"

"You want my honest opinion?"

"Of course."

"I don't trust him. Not one bit, but then he's not my family." Delta wiped an imaginary crumb off the table. "You gotta decide for yourself whether to believe him. Just know my Delta radar will be on full alert whenever he's around."

Jo grinned. "I wouldn't have it any other way."

The women chatted about Curtis's upcoming vet visit and set a time to meet in the common area to corral the kitten.

She started to head to her office when someone began pounding on the front door. "Are you expecting company first thing this morning?"

"Nope." Delta hurried out of the kitchen and to the front door with Jo trailing behind.

"It's Sheriff Franklin." Delta cautiously eased the door open.

"Good morning, Delta, Ms. Pepperdine." The sheriff tipped his hat. "I'm sorry to bother you so early, but I wondered if I could have a minute of your time."

"Of course." Jo motioned him into the living room.

"I got a fresh pot of coffee brewing and a batch of my banana nut bread I just pulled from the oven." Delta waited for him to step inside and then closed the door.

"Unfortunately, as much as I would love to partake of your delicious goodies, I'm here on official business."

Chapter 6

"I was hoping I could speak with one of your residents, Tara Cloyne."

"Tara." Jo shot Delta a quick glance. "She's not here. She left the farm yesterday morning."

"Do you know where she went?"

"My guess is she's on her way to Chicago, to her family. I've already contacted her probation officer, Ed Shevock."

The sheriff pulled a notepad and pen from his pocket. "You say she left here yesterday morning?"

"Actually, it may have been sometime the night before. She was having some emotional issues. Are you working with Mr. Shevock to try to locate her?"

"I'm not. I was hoping to speak to Ms. Cloyne about a former inmate she was acquainted with, Karen Griffin. She escaped from prison last night."

Delta let out a low whistle. "You think Tara may be involved in this woman's escape?"

"It's possible," the sheriff said. "I would like to take a look around her unit if you don't mind."

"No. Not at all. I'll go get the key." Jo grabbed her master keys and a jacket before returning to the living room. She led the sheriff out of the house and to Tara's unit. "We've already searched her room."

Delta joined them moments later, and the women stood in the doorway, watching.

"Can I ask the reason for Karen Griffin's incarceration?" Jo asked.

"It was all over the news last year. She was convicted of arson, insurance fraud and tampering with evidence."

"Whoo-ee." Delta hissed under her breath. "So this woman lit something on fire, and then filed an insurance claim?"

"In a nutshell."

"She was in a maximum-security prison for insurance fraud?" Jo shifted her feet.

"Insurance fraud was one element. Someone inside the residence perished as a result of the fire."

Delta pressed a hand to her chest. "How horrible."

"It was the woman's husband," the sheriff said. "That's only half of it. I'm sure you both know Harrison Cantwell."

"Unfortunately," Delta said.

"He's dead."

Jo looked incredulous. "Dead?"

"An area resident found his body in the alley behind the old movie theater this morning. Of course, the cause of death isn't known yet. Could be

Cantwell did himself in, but knowing him as I do, I suspect there's more to it than that."

"I met him yesterday during my first Divine Area Business Owner's meeting," Jo said.

"Which is another reason why I'm here. I heard about the meeting. I also caught wind he was ruffling a few feathers, including yours, so I figured I would drop by since you were one of the last people to have contact with him."

"Am I a suspect?" Jo asked. "I barely knew him."

"An eyewitness claims Harrison and you argued after he made some unsavory comments about the residents."

"That's true, but he was also rude to Pastor Murphy, Marlee, the Maltons and even Claire Harcourt."

"I heard that, as well. Which means I'm going to be a very busy man until we get to the bottom of what happened to him. Could you please repeat the conversation you had with Mr. Cantwell?"

Jo told him what she remembered about the brief and unpleasant exchange; how he commented that she was harboring hardened criminals and complained about the bakeshop employee. "I hate to speak ill of the dead, but he wasn't particularly charitable about raising money for the needy children's Christmas gifts."

"Can't say that I'm surprised," the sheriff said. "Pastor Murphy told me what you did; how you donated the money to cover the costs of the stolen toys and even offered to host a Santa's workshop here at the farm."

"I did, and we're looking forward to it. If you're in the area next Saturday evening, you should stop by."

"I might have to do that. In the meantime, if you hear from Ms. Cloyne, would you please give me a call?"

"Absolutely." A sudden thought popped into Jo's head. "You don't think the female escapee had something to do with Harrison's death, do you?"

"I'm not ruling anything or anyone out until the cause of death is determined. It could be coincidental, or there could be a connection," the sheriff said. "Your brother, Miles Parker, was helping Cantwell move some personal property. He was negotiating with him for the purchase of the movie theater."

"I heard he was," Jo said. "I'm guessing you've talked to Miles, as well."

"You are going to be busy," Delta said. "You sure you don't want me to pack up a couple of slices of banana nut bread for the road?"

"Now, Delta." The sheriff cracked the first smile since his arrival. "You do know how to twist a man's arm."

"That's what I thought. I'll meet you out on the front porch." Delta headed to the house while the sheriff waited for Jo to lock the door.

"I'm sure you can verify your whereabouts last evening," the sheriff said.

"I was here at the farm. We ate pizza, planned for the upcoming party and then we all turned in for the night."

"Alone?" the sheriff probed.

"Yes. Alone, if you don't count my dog, Duke. I'm a single woman."

"I don't mean to pry into your personal affairs, Ms. Pepperdine. I'm just doing my job."

"I'm sorry. I have my hands full, as well. A missing resident, a party for the kids on short notice, although that's my fault."

The sheriff and Jo reached his patrol car at the same time Delta emerged from the house carrying a brown paper bag. "I tossed in a couple of donuts in case you happen to run into that handsome son of yours, Deputy Brian."

"Thanks, Delta." Sheriff Franklin took the bag of goodies. "I appreciate your cooperation, Ms. Pepperdine. If you think of anything at all, please let me know."

"I will." Jo waited for the sheriff to climb into his patrol car and drive off. "Do you think Cantwell took his own life?"

"Not for a second." Delta shook her head. "The man was too ornery and stubborn, too self-centered to do something like that. My guess is he finally got on someone's last nerve. It angered them enough to take him out near his beloved theater."

"Which means Miles is also a suspect." Jo tapped her chin thoughtfully. "If he loved the theater so much, why would he agree to sell it to Miles?"

Delta rubbed her thumb and index finger together. "The only thing Harrison Cantwell loved more than his theater was money. If Miles offered him enough, the temptation would be too great."

"I hope they find the woman and figure out what happened to Cantwell." Jo climbed the steps and returned inside. She glanced at the clock on the fireplace mantle as they passed by. "What time is Curtis's vet appointment?"

"In half an hour. Goodness. Time got away from us. Go grab your shoes and purse while I rustle up a box for Curtis."

Jo flew up the stairs and found a pair of old slip-ons. She tossed her phone in her purse before hurrying back downstairs. Delta was in the kitchen, cutting holes in the side of a brown cardboard box. "I'll go grab Curtis and meet you out by the SUV."

"Sounds like a plan."

Jo made a beeline for the women's shared living area, where she found Kelli sweeping the kitchen floor. "I'm here to take Curtis to his first vet appointment."

"He's raring to go, at least he's raring to get out of the bathroom." Kelli eased the bathroom door open. "We didn't want him to wander off, so we kept him in there. He's been yowling all morning."

A black and white ball of fur barreled out of the room and skidded across the floor.

Jo swooped down and snatched him up. "You're not going to like the vet visit much better."

Curtis butted Jo's chin with the top of his head and then started to wiggle, anxious to be free. She tightened her grip. "This ought to be an adventure."

"Good luck." Kelli darted to the door and held it open. "I have a feeling he's not going to enjoy the car ride either."

"You're probably right, but it has to be done."

Doctor Block, a local vet, operated a clinic at his farm only a few miles from Jo's place. She found him after Duke hurt his paw jumping out of the bed of the pickup truck and took him to the vet to have it checked out.

Curtis and Jo caught up with Delta, who was waiting for them next to the SUV.

"We're gonna have to move fast." Delta set the box on the ground, flipped the flaps and smoothed the blanket she had placed in the bottom. "Ready when you are."

Curtis took one look at the box and began writing wildly, desperate to break free from Jo's ironclad hold. "Sorry, Curtis. This is for your own good." She eased him onto the blanket as Delta quickly closed the flaps.

YOWL. The sides of the box shook as a desperate Curtis attempted to escape.

"That went better than I expected." Delta carefully lifted the box while Jo opened the rear passenger door and waited for them to climb in.

MEOW. The yowls continued as a frantic Curtis tried to claw his way out of the top of the box.

"He's got a good set of lungs on him." Delta kept a firm grip on the box as Jo helped her buckle her seatbelt. "Good thing the vet is close by."

Jo jumped into the driver's seat and glanced in the rearview mirror. "Ready?"

"As we'll ever be," Delta quipped.

The SUV jostled along the driveway as Curtis's yowls grew louder.

"He sounds like he's being tortured."

"He ain't likin' this one little bit."

They reached the vet clinic, and Curtis grew quiet.

"Stay put, and I'll help you out." Jo sprinted to the rear passenger door.

Curtis's nose and whiskers pressed up against the small opening. "We're almost there. You're gonna be fine."

The kitten let out a pitiful meow.

"Poor thing. He hates riding." Jo led the way into the clinic and approached the front desk. "Curtis has an appointment with Doctor Block."

The woman consulted her clipboard. "Have you filled out Curtis's paperwork?"

"I did it online."

"Good. Then you're all set."

The women wandered to a row of empty seats near the window.

Jo leaned forward, watching Curtis's pink nose poke through the opening. "He sees the boxer over there." She pointed to a man seated in the back, a brown boxer sprawled out on the floor next to him.

"Yep." Delta nodded. "He's curious as a cat."

The man and the boxer were called first. A few minutes later, a woman holding a manila file folder emerged from the back. "Curtis, the kitty."

"That's us." Jo kept a tight grip on the box as the women followed her down the long hall.

"In here." The employee held the door and waited for them to step inside. "Doctor Block will be with you shortly."

Jo eased Curtis's box onto the counter. "You're such a good boy, Curtis. Delta will give you some extra treats when we get home," she cooed.

The vet arrived a short time later. "Hello, Jo. It's nice to see you again. How is Duke?"

"Duke is fine and loving life on the farm."

"Glad to hear it." The vet greeted Delta before motioning to the kitten, who was eyeing him suspiciously. "Is this Curtis?"

"It is. Curtis was a stray. Someone dropped him off at the farm, and he ended up adopting us."

"He's spoiled rotten," Delta added.

The vet motioned to the cat. "Do you mind?"

Jo handed him over.

"He appears to be in good health." The vet held Curtis close. "I would like to weigh him and take some measurements. It will give me a more accurate idea of his age."

Dr. Block excused himself and exited the examining room. He and Curtis were gone for several long moments before returning. The vet's expression was solemn, and Jo immediately suspected something was terribly wrong.

"I hope I'm not the bearer of bad news, but I discovered something about Curtis during my exam."

Chapter 7

Jo's heart skipped a beat. "Please don't tell me he has something seriously wrong with him. The women will be heartbroken."

"No," Doctor Block chuckled. "Unless you think they're going to mind that Curtis is a 'she.'"

"Well, mash my taters," Delta said.

Jo frowned. "Curtis is a female?"

"Yes, and she's a little younger than I first suspected. She isn't quite ready for spaying. We'll need to wait another month. I can give her the first set of vaccinations. Are you planning to keep Curtis?"

"Yes. Yes, of course," Jo nodded.

"Good." The vet appeared visibly relieved. "Some owners find their new pet isn't what they thought, and they decide they don't want to keep them."

"Curtis is part of the family," Delta chimed in.

"I'll administer the shots." He carried Curtis out of the room, and they returned a short time later. The vet handed her to Jo. "She took 'em like a real champ."

Dr. Block sat on a small stool. "I'll make an appointment for the spaying, and you can be on your way." He finished entering some notes on the laptop in front of him and then handed Jo a small card and a sheet of paper. "This is Curtis's next appointment and a list of reactions she may have because of the shots."

Jo thanked him for the information and placed Curtis back inside the box. The kitten let out a bloodcurdling cry when she flipped the flaps. "She doesn't like riding."

"Or the box," Delta said.

"Most cats don't." The vet accompanied them to the front desk and handed the receptionist Curtis's file before telling them good-bye.

Jo settled the bill, and the trio returned to the vehicle for the short drive home. "We'll wait to share Curtis's big surprise at dinner this evening," she said.

The ride home was as noisy as the ride to the vet with Curtis yowling loudly, making it impossible for the women to talk.

"We're here," Jo announced as they pulled into the driveway. "I think Curtis should hang out inside the house for the rest of the day so we can keep an eye on him...her."

"Good idea." Delta waited for Jo to help them out of the backseat. She led the way up the back steps, placed the box on the kitchen floor and carefully opened the top.

Duke, hearing the women return, trotted into the kitchen. He eyed Curtis warily as she leaped out of the box, stalked over to his doggie bed and sniffed the edge. Deeming it worthy of a closer inspection, she climbed on top and began pawing at the padding.

The pooch crossed the kitchen floor and let out a distressed whine.

"It's okay, Duke. We need to watch Curtis for a little while to make sure her shots don't make her sick." Jo bent down and patted his head.

Curtis finished investigating the doggie bed, hopped off and began heading in the direction of the dining room.

Delta shoved a hand on her hip. "I think she'll be fine."

"I think so, too."

The back door rattled, and Nash and Gary appeared. "We saw you come back. How was the vet appointment?"

"Curtis hated the car ride. My ears are still ringing from her yowling. Other than that, we're no worse for the wear," Jo joked.

"Her?" Nash lifted a brow.

"Curtis is a female cat. I figured we would tell the women at dinner tonight and let them decide if they want to pick a different name for her."

"Imagine that." Nash changed the subject. "Gary and I have been working on the sleigh and some other goodies for the kids' Christmas party. We already cut the frame for the sleigh but decided to show you what we have so far before moving full steam ahead with the details."

He placed several sketches on the table. "This one is the most promising. We need to make sure the frame is sturdy enough to support Santa and the gifts, but also something we can disassemble for easy storage."

"For use possibly next year?" Jo studied the sketches.

"Yeah." Nash nodded. "Of course, the decision is yours, Jo."

"If this turns out half as good as I think it will, we might make it an annual event." Jo's eyes shined. "I love it. I love them all. I'll let you decide which one to go with."

"Great," Gary said. "We'll start working on it now that we have your approval."

"Are you coming in for lunch?"

"We should probably make it a working lunch since we'll have to move fast to have everything ready by next week."

Woof. Duke, who had followed Curtis out of the kitchen, let out a warning bark. It was coming from the direction of the living room.

"The tree. Curtis!" Jo bolted from the kitchen and raced into the living room where she found Duke sprawled out in front of the Christmas tree, staring at it intently.

Delta, Nash and Gary were right behind her.

The tree stand rattled, and several branches began rustling. "Uh-oh." Jo parted the branches and peered inside. "Curtis?"

Two large, round eyes stared back at her.

"She's in the tree." Jo shoved her hand between the branches, the sharp pine needles stabbing her hand and arms. She leaned in as far as she dared, her fingertips grazing Curtis's underside. "Come here."

Not ready to vacate her newfound playground, Curtis scooted back and out of Jo's reach. "She thinks we're playing."

"I'll see if I can help." Nash dropped to his knees and crawled under the tree while Duke, captivated by Curtis's adventure, barked excitedly.

Jo caught another glimpse of Curtis's tail as she crept toward the base of the tree. "She's coming your way."

The tree shook, and a light shower of pine needles rained down on the tree skirt. "I got him...her." Nash rolled to the side and began inching his way back, Curtis firmly in his grasp.

"I'll take her."

Nash passed the cat to Gary before crawling the rest of the way out. He brushed the pine needles off his shirt. "Sorry about the pine needles."

"Don't worry about it. At least she didn't knock the tree over," Delta said. "I guess we're going to have to keep her out of here until she goes home."

"Naughty kitty," Jo scolded. "Although I can't blame her. It is a beautiful tree."

The men returned to the kitchen to retrieve their plans.

"What about supplies?" Jo asked. "Do you have enough materials?"

"I have plenty of plywood to finish cutting the frame today," Nash said. "I could use some new sheets of sandpaper and paint."

"I'll drive to town and pick up what you need. If you could make a list, I'll swing by and grab it before leaving."

"You're the best." Nash sneaked a quick kiss.

"Enough of the mushy stuff." Delta thrust a brown paper bag in Nash's direction. "You two need to get to work."

"Yes, ma'am." Gary followed Nash out the back door. Duke bolted past Jo and followed the men. "Duke's coming with you."

They waited for the pup to catch up. Nash gave Jo a thumbs up, and then the trio disappeared inside the workshop.

Jo returned to the kitchen, where she found Delta standing at the counter, frowning at something in her hand. "What's wrong?"

"Your cell phone was ringing. Then it stopped and started ringing again. It's a number I don't recognize. It looks like they left a message."

Jo took the phone from her. "I don't recognize the number either, but you're right. They left a message." She pressed her four-digit access code and held the phone to her ear.

Her eyes grew wide as she listened to the brief message. "You're not going to believe this."

Chapter 8

"I'll let you listen." Jo pressed the button to repeat the message.

"Jo. It's me, Tara. I wanted to let you know I'm okay. I'm sorry about leaving so suddenly. I don't fit in at the farm. I mean, everyone was nice, but I felt trapped. I hope you can forgive me. Tell everyone I said 'good-bye.'"

The call ended.

Delta placed a hand on her hip. "She's got herself in a mess of trouble. Does she even realize how much trouble this is gonna cause her?"

"Should I call her back?"

"I would let her probation officer handle it," Delta said.

"You're right. I'll copy the number and send it to him now. I'll send a copy to Sheriff Franklin, too." Jo grew quiet as she tapped the screen. "I guess this means we have an opening again."

"The decision is yours, but I would wait 'til after Christmas if I were you."

"My thoughts exactly. It will be too hard to try to bring in a new resident right now." Jo sighed heavily.

Delta patted her friend's arm. "Don't beat yourself up over this, Jo. You tried. You did your best. You can't save everybody."

"Tara never did seem to like living here." Jo lifted her gaze, staring thoughtfully out the window. "I'm gonna run next door and grab Nash and Gary's shopping list and then head to town."

She found the men inside the workshop, the sound of a table saw buzzing loudly. The smell of fresh sawdust filled the air. It took a minute for Jo to catch Nash's attention. The workshop grew quiet. "Hey, pretty lady."

Jo's cheeks warmed at the offhanded compliment. "I thought I would run over to the hardware store and grab your supplies now instead of later. I don't want to be responsible for slowing production in Santa's workshop. I have another errand in town and figured I could take care of them at the same time."

She pointed at the thick wooden cutout the men were working on, the rounded edges swirling up, creating the outline of a sleigh. "What color will the sleigh runners be?"

"The runners will be black. Thanks for the reminder. I forgot to add black paint." Nash pulled a piece of paper from his shirt pocket and grabbed a pen. "Red for the sleigh, black for the runners and I think some touches of white trim will do the trick." He finished writing and handed the list to Jo. "I forgot to mention it before, but I saw Sheriff

Franklin here this morning. Was he asking about Tara?"

"Sort of," Jo said. "There's been a recent prison escape. The woman's name is Karen something. She and Tara were friends. The sheriff was hoping to question Tara about her."

"Do you think they're together?" Gary asked. "The women, I mean?"

Jo shrugged. "Could be. Speaking of Tara, she called me from the Tracfone. I'll let you listen to her message." She pulled the cell phone from her purse, turned it on and pressed the play button.

Nash waited until the message ended. "At least she had the decency to apologize. What do you think will happen to her?"

"She'll be caught and returned to Central to finish out her sentence. I wonder if the judge will add more time if they find out she helped her friend escape. Either way, I think she made a terrible mistake," Jo said. "That's not all. Harrison Cantwell was found dead behind his movie theater."

Gary dropped the piece of wood he was holding. "Cantwell's dead? What happened?"

"A local found him in the alley behind the old theater. He was at our Divine business meeting yesterday. He said some unkind and untrue things about the residents. We had a few words, and I'm guessing if they determine he was murdered, I'm a suspect," Jo shifted her purse to her other arm. "Me, Marlee, the Maltons, Claire. Even Pastor Murphy."

"I doubt the man did himself in," Nash said. "He was too ornery to take his own life. He thrived on making people miserable."

"There was one person who seemed to have gotten under his skin during the meeting yesterday, it was Carrie Ford."

"I'm not surprised about that." Nash shook his head. "There was no love lost between Carrie and Harrison."

"Was he an ex?" Jo asked.

"No. Carrie's last husband, Abner, and Harrison were friends. Well, drinking buddies. They hung out at the Half Wall bar over in Four Corners."

"And Carrie didn't care for Harrison," Jo guessed.

"Not at all. Abner would get restless every so often and take off with Harrison. Carrie always knew who he was with and where to find him. The last incident ended badly. Carrie confronted them at the bar and told Abner it was time to go home. Harrison got in her face, told her to be a good little wife and run on home."

"Ah." Jo lifted a brow. "And Carrie didn't appreciate the comment."

"That's an understatement. I heard she cussed him out and stormed out of the bar. Carrie denies it, but someone punctured Harrison's car tires. Hours later, the men stumbled out of the bar and found four flat tires. Harrison was furious. He and Abner bummed a ride from someone. They went back to Abner and Carrie's place where Harrison confronted her."

Jo's eyes grew wide. "What happened?"

"It got ugly. Abner ended up calling the cops. Harrison was arrested for assault and trespassing. The incident ended their friendship. I think Abner was afraid Carrie would use his taxidermy tools on him."

"She doesn't strike me as having a temper."

"Harrison has a way of sending even mild-mannered people over the edge," Nash said. "What's Carrie up to these days?"

"She has a unique marketing strategy for her taxidermy business."

"That oughta keep her busy," Nash said. "What's unique about it?"

Jo thought about Myron, the blackbird. "It's hard to describe. She's renamed it Carrie's Custom Creations. Let's just say the business mascot is a talking blackbird named Myron."

"Sounds intriguing."

"I'll have Carrie bring Myron by sometime so you can see for yourself." Jo tucked Nash's list in the side pocket of her purse. "I need to get going."

She stepped out of the workshop and was halfway to her SUV when Raylene flagged her down. "Hey, Jo."

Jo waited for her to catch up.

"How is Curtis?" Raylene asked. "How did the vet appointment go?"

"It was...interesting. I have some news but want to wait until dinnertime so I can tell everyone at once."

A concerned look crossed Raylene's face. "Is Curtis all right?"

"Curtis is fine." Jo patted her purse. "I'm on my way to the hardware store to pick up some supplies for the sleigh and Santa's workshop."

"Before you go, I need to show you something."

Jo followed Raylene to the public restrooms located between the store and the bakeshop. It was a compact space with two separate unisex bathrooms. There were vending machines in the corner. One was filled with water and sodas and the other filled with snacks. "Someone tried to break into the machine."

"Which one?" Jo asked.

"The snack vending machine."

Jo stepped forward to inspect the plexiglass. Sure enough, there were several deep gouges on the side of the frame. "It looks like they stuck a screwdriver or something in there, trying to break it."

"I didn't notice it last night when I cleaned the bathrooms. I'm not sure when it happened."

"Have you asked the other women about it?"

"Yeah," Raylene said, "they have no idea. I was on my way over to tell Nash about it when I saw you, so I figured I would show it to you first."

"I'll handle it from here." Jo thanked Raylene and then returned to the workshop.

"Back already?" Nash teased.

"I need to show you something." She led Nash and Gary to the damaged vending machine. "Raylene said she noticed it first thing this morning. Someone was trying to open it."

Nash ran his hand along the edge. "Unfortunately, there's not much I can do. You'll have to contact the vendor to order a replacement."

Jo thanked them for looking at it and headed to her vehicle. During the drive to town, she mulled over Tara's mysterious call. Why had she called? Perhaps she was regretting her decision and hoped to return to the farm.

It was too late for that. She would have to go before a judge if – or when – she was caught.

Jo found a parking spot in front of Tool Time Hardware and made her way inside. Wayne Malton was in the back, helping a customer. She gave him a quick wave, grabbed a shopping cart and headed to the paint department.

She found the perfect shade of red to match Santa's red suit and placed the can of paint, along with a quart of white and black paint in her shopping cart.

"Working on your Santa's workshop project already?" Wayne stepped in behind her.

"As a matter of fact, I have a list." Jo handed Nash's list to him.

"We stock all of this." Wayne walked the store aisles, assembling the items on the list and then carried them to the checkout counter as Jo trailed behind. "I'm sure you heard about Harrison Cantwell's death."

"I have. Sheriff Franklin was on my front step first thing this morning."

Jo waited for Wayne to finish ringing up her purchases before sliding her debit card through the machine. "If Cantwell's death is ruled suspicious, we'll all be under scrutiny."

"You, me, Claire, Marlee, Pastor Murphy and your half-brother, Miles."

"Don't forget about Carrie. If we're talking motive, Carrie would be right at the tippy top of the list," Jo said. "As far as Miles goes, the sheriff will probably quickly clear him."

"Maybe not. Miles had access to the theater." Wayne explained how Cantwell had visited the hardware store a couple of days ago to purchase a combination lock. He told Wayne he was installing the lock because he hired Miles to help him clear out some of his personal belongings.

"And he gave Miles access to the building? That sounds out of character for the man."

"It's because Miles promised him an earnest money deposit for the purchase. You can tell me to mind my own business, but I'm guessing he used some of his settlement money for the purchase," Wayne said.

"No." Jo shook her head. "I haven't given Miles a dime. We're still working out the details of our agreement."

"Well, according to what Cantwell told me, Miles planned to get the cash from somewhere." Wayne tucked the receipt in one of the bags. "I'll help you carry these to your car."

When they reached the vehicle, Wayne placed the items in the back. "He's probably still there."

"Who?"

"Miles. I saw him hanging around the theater this morning when the crime scene investigators were there."

123

"Thanks for the info." Jo waited for Wayne to return to the store and slowly made her way to the theater at the other end of the street.

The front of the majestic old theater sported gold-colored columns on each side. A ticket booth was between the double doors.

She stepped closer and peered through the glass pane. Dim light beamed out. Jo wandered to the side entrance. She tried the door and was surprised to find it was unlocked.

"Hello?" Jo took a tentative step inside. She spotted Miles standing near the movie poster display case.

He paused for a moment before making his way to the door. "Hello, Joanna."

"I had an errand to run in town. Wayne at the hardware store told me you were here." Jo shifted awkwardly. "Do you have a minute?"

"Of course."

Jo hesitated, not sure of exactly where to start. "Mr. Cantwell is dead. Are the authorities…"

"They're still out back, investigating."

"And they're letting you hang out here?"

"They already searched this place top to bottom. I was the one who let them in."

"Do you know what happened?" Jo asked.

Miles shoved his hands in his pockets. "I…I probably shouldn't be telling you this, but he died from a gunshot wound."

"Self-inflicted?"

"I don't know. I overheard one of the investigators talking about it." Miles motioned for Jo to follow him through the double set of doors and into the main theater. "I have a feeling you aren't here to discuss Harrison Cantwell."

"I'm not. I figured I would stop by to clear the air and to let you know I've given our conversation some serious thought."

Chapter 9

Jo continued. "I accept your apology. We were both understandably shocked by your discovery. I can only imagine how you must've felt after finding out who your father was."

"And I understand how you must've felt when I showed up on your doorstep claiming to be your half-brother," Miles said.

"So, I figured we could start over. Perhaps we can even reach a mutual agreement on the settlement."

Miles lifted his hands as he spun in a slow circle. "Which would get me that much closer to fulfilling a dream."

"This," Jo said. "Your dream is to own this movie theater."

"Precisely."

"But Cantwell is dead. The property could be tied up in probate or turned over to the heirs and they might decide not to sell."

"Possibly," Miles admitted. "I'm a bit of a gambler. I'm willing to hang around and see what happens next. If I'm lucky, maybe the heirs will decide to sell this place lock, stock and barrel and include the storage area around back, too."

"Storage area?" Jo asked.

"Yeah. Cantwell specifically excluded the storage area. He kept mentioning some sort of secret stash. I think he was making it up, but who knows," Miles shrugged. "As wily as the guy was, nothing about him would surprise me."

"I still don't understand why you want to move here. There are a million other small towns and certainly dozens of other old movie theaters you could purchase."

"Like I mentioned before, Divine is as close to home as anything. I have no family in California.

Sure, I have a few friends, but the cost of living?" Miles blew air through thinned lips. "My settlement won't last long. It's much more affordable here, not to mention the fresh air, the wide-open spaces and then there's you."

"It's..."

"Before you outright shoot me down, I want to show you around this place." Miles excitedly motioned for Jo to follow him. "This theater is a piece of history."

Despite the thought of Cantwell's recent demise, Jo couldn't disagree. The interior was magnificent with its second-story VIP side boxes. The tiered seating was intimate yet spacious. Front and center was a large projection screen.

They circled the theater floor and returned to the front lobby. "Well? Now that we've made amends, would you reconsider the stipulation that I leave the area?"

"Forgiving is one thing." Jo clasped her hands. "Let me think about it."

"Fair enough. If you do agree, I would entertain the idea of bringing you on board as a business partner."

Jo laughed. "One thing at a time. I haven't said I'm removing the stipulation. Besides, I have my hands full with my current businesses."

"Sorry if I come across as pushy." Miles gazed dreamily around the lobby. "I haven't been this excited in a long time. I guess I'm getting a little carried away."

"We should all be passionate about something." Jo promised Miles she would consider his request...and offer, and then exited the building. She returned to her vehicle and started to climb inside when she spotted Claire entering her antique shop.

Jo backtracked, crossing to the other side of the street.

The store's overhead bell chimed, and Claire stepped out from the back. "Hey, Jo. I thought I saw your vehicle in front of the hardware store."

"I'm picking up supplies for Santa's workshop." Jo told her friend how excited Nash, Gary, Delta and the women were at the thought of hosting the children.

"You're gonna make some needy children very happy."

"I hope so."

Claire motioned toward Main Street. "You heard about Harrison Cantwell's death?"

"Yes. I just left the old theater. Cantwell had hired Miles to help him pack up some items not included in the sale of the property. He showed me around, except for the spot out back where Harrison's body was found."

"I heard he was found on the back stoop." Claire pressed a hand to her throat. "I never cared for the man, but I didn't want to see him dead."

"Me, either."

"You said you were with Miles?"

"I was." Jo briefly told her friend about Miles's surprise visit to the farm, his apology and his desire to stay in Divine.

"A movie buff? Huh. Maybe he took Cantwell out," Claire theorized. "He had plenty of opportunities."

"But what would be the motive? I doubt Cantwell willed the property to him on his death."

"True. Well, if Harrison's death wasn't accidental or suicide, Sheriff Franklin has more than his share of suspects."

Jo changed the subject. "What are you doing for Christmas, Claire?"

"My sister, who lives in Smithville, invited me to dinner. I'm not sure if I'm gonna go. She's got her hands full with children and grandchildren. I always feel like I'm imposing. I'm tempted to hang out at home, pop a frozen turkey dinner in the microwave, watch the parade and doze off in my recliner."

"That's a terrible Christmas Day plan. Why don't you come to the farm? Although I can't guarantee it will be any less chaotic than your sister's place."

"I..." Claire met Jo's gaze. "I don't want to impose."

"We would love to have you," Jo insisted. "The more, the merrier."

"Okay." Claire nodded, a smile lighting her face. "I accept your invitation."

"Good. Christmas dinner is at one. Plan to come early for stockings, and perhaps even old Saint Nick will stop by for a visit."

"Gary?" Claire guessed.

"The one and only. He and Nash are up to their elbows in workshop construction." Jo consulted her watch. "Speaking of that, I need to get the supplies for the sleigh back to the North Pole."

Claire followed her to the door. "If I didn't know better, I would say God sent his own special angel right here to the tiny town of Divine, and her name is Jo."

"There are times I don't feel particularly saintly." She thought about her anger directed at Harrison Cantwell when he taunted her.

"You're as close as they come," Claire insisted. "I don't know how you found Divine out of all of the places in the world, but I'm glad you did."

"I knew the moment I laid eyes on the farm that this was going to be my home and that God had picked out a very special place for me to live out the rest of my days." Jo could feel the back of her eyes burn. "Little did I know he would also bless me with such a wonderful group of special friends."

Claire made a coughing sound. "We're getting all sappy. You better get out of here before we both start bawling our eyes out."

"I'm on my way." Jo impulsively hugged her friend and darted out of the shop, counting her blessings and thanking God for her friends.

On the drive home, her thoughts turned to Miles Parker, how excited he seemed as he showed her around the theater. She knew exactly how he felt. She had felt the same way the first time she'd laid eyes on the farm. It was love at first sight.

Jo was able to see beyond the dilapidated buildings, the outdated Victorian and the overgrown fields. She had a vision, not unlike she guessed Miles's vision for the old theater.

Was it an act? What if Miles had murdered Harrison Cantwell? But for what purpose? He had the opportunity, but what was the motive?

Miles was a smart man, and Jo was sure he knew he would be a prime suspect if the authorities determined someone had murdered Cantwell.

Back at the farm, she dropped the purchases off at the workshop and returned to the house. Jo stepped inside and was greeted by loud yowling. Delta and Sherry stood at the kitchen counter, lined with stainless steel mixing bowls.

"What's all that racket?" Jo shrugged out of her jacket and hung it on the hook near the door.

"Curtis is driving us crazy. The cat is bound and determined to get back to the Christmas tree." Delta motioned to Duke, who was in the dining room, watching from the other side of the makeshift barricade.

"Duke is having a grand old time watching Curtis throw hissy fits."

The cat yowled again. "Shush before Delta locks you in the cellar."

Jo laughed. "You're not going to lock Curtis in the cellar."

"I might. How did it go?"

"While I was in town, I stopped by to chat with Claire and invited her to Christmas dinner."

"Is she gonna come? I think she has a sister somewhere close by."

"She does, but it sounds like chaos at her sister's place. I offered her an alternative, to come and spend Christmas with us, not that it will be less chaotic." Jo tapped Sherry's shoulder. "You finished your shift at the deli?"

"We didn't have any Christmas luncheons booked, so Marlee told me I could leave early."

"Any news on Harrison's death?" Delta asked.

"Yes. As a matter of fact, there is." Jo told them about her visit to the movie theater, quickly glossing over her chat with Miles. Nothing got past Delta, and she gave Jo a knowing look, which meant after Sherry left, she planned to drill down on the details of their conversation.

"He showed me around, but we didn't go to the alley out back where Cantwell's body was found."

"I was thinking about it," Delta reached for a mixing spoon. "I'm still stumped over how Miles had access to the property. I know Harrison Cantwell well enough to know he wouldn't be handing out keys willy nilly to just anyone."

"Unless Miles forked over cash to secure the property."

"And how did he get the money?" Delta waved the spoon in Jo's direction.

"That's a good question. I didn't ask Miles if he gave Cantwell cash." Jo grew quiet, wondering how much she should share about Miles's desire to remain in Divine. She was still on the fence about the matter. Accepting an apology and moving on was one thing. Having the man as a neighbor and living nearby was something entirely different.

She shifted the conversation to a safer topic. "What's for dinner? It smells delicious."

"We're having my pasta extravaganza. The lasagna is bubbling away in the oven. Sherry and I are working on filling goodie jars."

"Don't forget we're sharing our big news about Curtis during dinner." Jo opened the silverware drawer and began counting out forks.

"I heard Curtis has a secret," Sherry said. "The other women and I have been trying to guess, but so far, we can't figure it out."

"You'll find out soon enough," Jo promised.

"Hang on. Here comes tomorrow's weather." Delta grabbed the television's remote off the counter. "I like to watch the weather, especially now that we're gettin' into the snow and freezing rain season."

The trio grew silent as Delta watched the local meteorologist give a rundown of the days ahead. "It's gonna be spittin' a little of the wet-freezing stuff. We better stock up on salt for the sidewalks."

She started to turn the volume down when a breaking news alert flashed across the bottom of the screen.

"Wait." Jo held up a hand. "I wonder if they're going to report on Cantwell's death."

A news anchor appeared. In the lower corner of the screen flashed a picture of a woman, her brown hair pulled back in a ponytail and a sullen expression on her face.

"We have an update on the breaking news story out of Smith County. Central State Women's Penitentiary is on lockdown pending the investigation into the escape of Karen Griffin."

The reporter went on to say the authorities believed the woman had help from someone on the outside and was asking anyone who may have seen or heard from her to call the state police's hotline number.

"Guess they're keeping the fact the woman set her house on fire, killed her husband and tried to collect his life insurance out of the news." Delta turned the volume down. "I bet Central is pure chaos right about now."

"You worked at the prison for a number of years. Do you remember any prison escapes?" Jo asked.

"No escapes, but there were several riots and protests. I'm betting the authorities are right, and the woman had some outside help."

"You know what?" Sherry's eyes were still glued to the television screen. "I recognize her.

Chapter 10

"The woman they showed…the one who escaped from the prison." Sherry pointed at the television screen. "I saw her in the deli yesterday. At least, I'm pretty sure it was her."

"What did she do?" Jo asked.

"She was asking a bunch of questions."

Delta stepped closer. "What kinda questions?"

"About us. About this place."

A cold chill jolted Jo. "You're kidding."

"It's not unusual for someone to ask me about the farm, but it's mostly locals, someone who lives in the area and is curious about how things work. She was different. I've never seen her before yesterday."

Delta grasped Sherry's arm. "Tell us everything you know."

Sherry told them that it was early in the morning and that the woman had sat at a table in the corner and near the door. "She ordered a coffee and a donut. I felt sorry for her because she was counting out change to pay the bill, so I told her I would pay for the food. That's when we got to talking, and she asked about the farm."

"We need to call Sheriff Franklin." Jo dashed to her office and grabbed her cell phone. "Yes, I would like to be transferred to Sheriff Franklin or whoever is investigating Karen Griffin's escape."

There was a brief pause before the sheriff came on the line. "Sheriff Franklin speaking."

"This is Joanna Pepperdine. Sherry Marshall, my resident who works at Divine Delicatessen, recognized Karen Griffin from a mugshot they showed on the television. Yes. Sherry is here now. Thank you. Good-bye."

Jo waved the phone in the air. "The sheriff is on his way."

"I..." Sherry clasped her hands. "You don't think he'll believe I had anything to do with this woman."

"No." Jo started to pace. "But Tara knew her. They were friends."

Delta set the remote on the windowsill. "Wouldn't it be something if Tara and this woman were hanging around here."

Jo thought about Tara's phone call. "I still have Tara's Tracfone number."

"Maybe you should try to call her," Delta said.

"Or wait for Sheriff Franklin."

The sheriff arrived a short time later. Delta answered the door and led him into the kitchen where Jo and Sherry waited.

Sherry repeated the story about the woman showing up at the deli and asking questions about the farm.

The sheriff jotted down notes as Sherry talked. "I felt sorry for her. She seemed a little down on her luck, so I paid for her coffee and donut."

"And you're saying she looked like the woman in the news report?" the sheriff prompted.

"Yes. Her hair wasn't pulled back in a ponytail, but I'm almost positive it was the same woman. Oh my gosh." Sherry's eyes grew wide. "Her hair was kind of across her face. She had a bruise." She pointed at her cheek. "It was right there."

"Did you happen to notice which way she went when she left?"

Sherry reluctantly shook her head. "No. I got busy with other customers, and I didn't see her leave."

"What if Tara and Karen are together?" Jo asked.

"I've already spoken to Officer Shevock, Tara's probation officer," the sheriff replied. "He's attempted to reach her several times. No one answers."

"Maybe she recognizes the probation officer's number, and that's why she isn't answering," Delta said. "What if Jo tried?"

"Are you up for it?" the sheriff asked.

"Yes. What should I say?"

"Keep the conversation casual. Let her know you're concerned for her safety. Perhaps she'll slip and give you a clue to her whereabouts."

"Should I ask her about Karen Griffin?"

"Not specifically. Ask her if she's safe and alone and if she made it to Illinois."

Jo juggled the phone in her hands. "I'm sure she already knows I gave the cell phone number to her probation officer."

"So she might not even answer," Delta said.

"Maybe not, but it's worth a try." Jo sucked in a breath as she scrolled the screen, searching for the number Tara had called from. The call went to voice mail. "Hi, Tara. It's Jo. I'm concerned about you.

Please call me when you have time. Thanks." Jo ended the call.

The sheriff asked Sherry a few more questions, and then Jo walked him to the door. "Is there any news on Harrison Cantwell's death?"

"I've questioned several people who were among the last to see him alive. He gave no indication he was under duress or concerned for his safety. I should have more information after the autopsy is complete." Sheriff Franklin thanked Jo for the phone call and stepped onto the front porch. "You may want to keep an eye out for the escapee. If Sherry is correct and the woman showed up at the deli, she seems mighty curious about you. I'll set up extra patrols in the area, as well."

"We'll be keeping an eye out," Jo promised. "This morning, we noticed that someone tried to break into one of our vending machines. I thought it might have been kids. Now I'm wondering if it was someone else."

"Do you mind if I take a look?"

"Of course not." Jo joined him on the porch. They fell into step as they made their way to the front of the businesses and to the small area near the public restrooms. "This is it."

"It looks like they used a screwdriver or something with a flat head to try to pop out the front panel." The sheriff stepped closer. "Doesn't look like they got too far."

"No."

Sheriff Franklin straightened. "Like I said, I'll schedule additional patrols for the area, particularly at night."

They returned to the sheriff's patrol car. "I appreciate the call. If you think of anything else or experience any other suspicious incidents, please don't hesitate to call."

"I can assure you that you're at the top of my list. If I hear back from Tara, I'll let you know what she says."

The sheriff drove off, and Jo returned to the kitchen. Tinted mason jars lined the counter. "What are you working on?"

"Delta's Divine Granola. I've been tweaking a new recipe for homemade Christmas gifts. Since you're here, I'd like to borrow your taste buds."

"I love granola."

Delta grabbed a large spoon from the drawer and handed it to her. "Get an ample sample."

Jo dipped the clean spoon inside the large mixing bowl. She inspected the contents before shaking a generous amount into her cupped hand. "What's in it?"

"Everything but the kitchen sink," Delta joked. "It has almonds, pecans, walnuts, rolled oats and my secret ingredient. I'll let you take a guess."

Jo tossed the handful of granola in her mouth and began chewing. "Peanuts?"

"It has peanuts, but that's not my secret ingredient."

"It has a hint of sweet." Jo squinted her eyes and studied the rest of what was left on the spoon. "Coconut."

Delta playfully whacked her friend's arm. "You cheated."

"I did." Jo grinned. "It's delicious." She motioned to the jars. "So, you're going to fill the jars with your delicious granola and give them out as gifts?"

"I am." Delta filled one of the smaller jars. She secured the lid and then reached for a roll of red ribbon sporting smiling snowmen. She tied the ribbon around the rim of the lid. "Voila! Instant homemade gifts. I'm gonna give one to Marlee, Pastor Murphy, Claire, the Maltons over at the hardware store. Can you think of anyone else?"

"Me," Jo laughed. "You could also give one to our neighbor, Dave Kilwin."

"I forgot about Dave." Delta reached for the piece of paper next to the jars and scribbled his name on it. "Good idea."

"Speaking of Pastor Murphy, I wonder when he's stopping by to drop off the kid's Christmas lists and the first round of presents."

"Delta Childress." Delta smacked her forehead. "I plum forgot. He called earlier. He said he should be here around seven, right after dinner."

"That will work out perfectly. We can eat, clean up and then start wrapping the presents. We'll be experts by the time this season ends." Jo set the spoon in the sink. "I ordered the Santa suit, Mrs. Claus suit and elves' outfits first thing this morning and paid for expedited delivery. They'll be here tomorrow."

"Giving me plenty of time to make a few minor adjustments if they don't quite fit right," Delta said.

"Better you than me. You don't want to know how horrible my sewing skills are." Jo set the table while Sherry and Delta finished filling and decorating the mason jars. The residents, along with Gary and Nash, trickled in.

Dinner was a festive affair, with Nash and Gary reporting they made excellent progress on Santa's sleigh.

"Which reminds me, Pastor Murphy will be here after dinner with the first load of gifts. We can start wrapping after we eat," Jo said. "With all of us working together, we should be able to knock it out in no time."

Curtis, who sat eyeing them from the other side of the temporary barricade, meowed loudly.

"Poor Curtis. I think he's ready to go home." Michelle stepped over the barricade and reached down to pat his head.

"I wouldn't put too many Christmas decorations out if I were you. The stinker already climbed the tree once. Speaking of Curtis, Delta and I have an announcement." Jo waited for the others to finish

151

clearing the table and gather in the living room before grabbing Curtis and joining them. "As all of you know, today was Curtis's first visit to the vet."

"He looks like he made it through the shots without any trouble," Sherry said.

"The vet gave us some interesting news," Jo motioned to Delta. "You tell them."

"Curtis is a she."

"Huh?" Raylene frowned.

"The vet informed Delta and me that Curtis is a female."

"You're kidding?" Kelli burst out laughing.

"The question is...do we change Curtis's name?"

"I think it would confuse Curtis," Kelli shook her head. "He...she already answers to the name."

"Me too," Leah said.

"I think Curtis is a good name, whether it's a he or she," Raylene chimed in.

"Then it's settled." Jo passed the cat to Leah, who was closest. "Why don't you take her home, and then we'll head over to the workshop to check out Nash and Gary's progress and wait for Pastor Murphy."

The women began filing out of the house. Raylene was the last to leave. "Any word from Tara?"

"She left a message on my cell phone, apologizing. I tried calling her back, but she didn't answer." Jo slowly shook her head. "It's like she vanished into thin air."

"With a cell phone. I'm sure she had some help."

"I thought the same thing." Jo glanced around and lowered her voice. "A woman escaped from the prison yesterday. According to Sheriff Franklin, the escapee and Tara were friends."

Raylene's eyes grew wide. "What if Tara helped her escape?"

"If she did, they're both in big trouble. Not only that, Sherry recognized the woman. She showed up at the deli, asking questions about the farm."

"You don't think this woman is hanging around here, do you?"

"I don't know what to think. Sheriff Franklin promised to set up extra nighttime patrols in the area."

Raylene pressed the palms of her hands together. She opened her mouth to say something and then quickly closed it.

"What were you going to say?" Jo asked.

"Just that Tara liked to talk the big talk."

"About moving to New York and becoming a famous makeup artist?"

"That and other stuff."

"Spit it out," Jo said. "What did she say?"

"You're loaded," Raylene blurted out. "She did some digging around on the internet about you. She

154

always wondered why you opened your farm to house former female convicts."

"So she did some digging around, found out about my past and told you about it."

"She did." Raylene hurried on. "It isn't any of my business."

"No, it's not. What's done is done," Jo sighed. "Do you think what she said was significant?"

"Only that if she was telling us you had a lot of money, she might have been telling others."

"Like her friend, the prison escapee." Jo thought about the damaged vending machine. "If the woman is hanging around here starting to cause trouble, it's only a matter of time before she tries something else."

A beam of bright headlights flashed across the side of the house. "Pastor Murphy is here." On the way out, Jo locked the doors. The women reached the barn and began unloading the gifts from the pastor's van.

"This should keep us busy for a while," Jo joked.

"There's more where these came from." The pastor pulled a bicycle from the back and handed it to Nash. "I figure two more loads should do it. I have some news to share, but I'll wait until we're all done."

"Good news or bad news?" Jo reached for a stack of board games.

"Let's just say it's interesting news."

They made quick work of placing the rest of the toys in front of the makeshift workbenches Nash and Gary had assembled from leftover sheets of plywood.

Delta put Sherry in charge of tracking the gifts and recipients. The rest of the women wrapped while the men loaded the presents in large trash bags and then placed the bags in a bin in the corner.

Jo ran next door to Nash's workshop and returned with his portable radio. She plugged it in and searched the stations until she found Christmas music.

It didn't take long for them to finish wrapping the gifts, tagging them and placing them in the bins. Delta headed to the house, returning a short time later with hot chocolate and frosted sugar cookies.

Jo grabbed a cookie and motioned to Pastor Murphy. "What's the news you promised to share?"

"You're not going to believe it. It's a Christmas miracle," the pastor said.

Chapter 11

"You found your missing toys," Jo guessed.

"I wish. That would be a Christmas miracle. Harrison Cantwell sent me a check for the children's toys."

Jo blinked rapidly. "He did?"

"Two hundred dollars."

"He didn't seem sympathetic to the cause the other day."

"Maybe God finally got to his heart before it was too late."

"Amen to that," Delta said.

"Which means I don't need all of this." The pastor reached into his pocket and pulled out the check Jo had written to replace the stolen toys.

"Please keep it. Put whatever is leftover toward the children's gifts for next year."

"Are you sure?"

"Positive. Why do you think Harrison Cantwell decided to help out?"

The pastor shrugged. "I have no idea. He was a hard, bitter man. I'm surprised your brother was working with him."

"Reading between the lines of what Miles told me, he was dangling the carrot that he planned to purchase the property. My guess is Miles's offer was substantial." Jo crossed her arms. "I have a hard time believing Harrison may have taken his own life."

"I don't think he shot himself."

"Why not?" Jo asked.

The pastor hesitated. "Talk around town is he had injuries to his hands and arms."

"Were they injuries you would get if you tried to ward off an attacker?"

"I don't know." The pastor shrugged. "I'm sure we're all in for another round of questioning since we were among the last to see him at the DABO meeting. Carrie Ford is upset. She stopped by the church just before I left."

"Upset?"

"I...I shouldn't have said anything. Pastor confidentiality and all. Forgive my moment of indiscretion."

"Maybe it's because she's also on the investigator's radar."

"Perhaps. She never would tell me what upset her. Again, I've said too much."

"I understand," Jo said. "I would never ask you to reveal confidential information about someone."

As Jo followed him to his van, the pastor promised to bring another load of gifts the following evening.

"Thank you for everything, Jo." The pastor glanced back at the workshop. "You've got a great group of residents. I know I say it every time, but I'm impressed with what you've been able to accomplish."

"Thank you. Your opinion means a lot to me. It's a labor of love."

He shifted his gaze, his eyes meeting Jo's eyes. "What are you going to do about the opening?"

"I plan to wait until after the holidays to start thinking about adding a new resident."

The pastor closed the van door and rolled down the window. "Let me know when you're ready. I have a couple of women who are scheduled for release soon that I think would be good candidates."

"I wish I had more room," Jo said wistfully.

"You're making a big difference in six...five women's lives."

"Sometimes I wonder; especially considering what happened with Tara."

"Tara was short-sighted. You can't help someone unless they want to be helped."

"True. She had so much potential. What's done is done. I'll see you tomorrow." Jo stepped away from the van and returned to the barn as the pastor drove off.

The women were packing up the wrapping supplies. "While you're all here, there's something I want to talk about."

Jo briefly told them about the prison escapee and that Sherry had remembered seeing the woman at the deli. "Sherry said she seemed curious about the farm. I'm not sure if this has anything to do with the damage to the vending machine, but we must be on guard. Please do not wander around outside at night. If you need to go out, use the buddy system."

Gary waited for Jo to finish. "And I thought I saw someone running out behind the building last night."

Leah rubbed the sides of her arms. "Do you think it was Tara or the woman who escaped?"

"We don't know," Jo confessed. "They were friends. What I do know is that Tara still has a key to her room."

"I'll change out the door lock to her room tomorrow," Nash said. "We can change the code for the common area's keyless entry right now."

Jo had recently installed a keyless door entry at Nash's suggestion, which helped eliminate having to keep multiple copies of keys for each of the residents.

"I wouldn't mind camping out in our living room until they catch the woman," Kelli said.

"Me either," Leah said. "At least we would be together."

"Does anyone else feel unsafe and want to stick together until the authorities apprehend the woman?" Jo asked.

The rest of the residents raised their hands.

Jo turned to Nash. "Do you still have the set of walkie-talkies?"

"I do. I'll go get them." Nash strode out of the barn, returning moments later with the walkie-talkies in hand. "The women can keep one of them. I'll keep the other. If you see or hear anything, you can give me a call."

Jo was visibly relieved. "That's a great idea."

With a plan in place, Nash escorted the women to their units. He waited while they gathered their personal belongings and made their way into the common area. While he kept watch, Gary, Jo and Delta began gathering bedding and mattresses and carried them to the living room.

Curtis, who was happy to be home, pranced back and forth, watching them arrange the bedding.

Kelli was the last straggler. She dropped her pillows and blankets on top of her mattress. "We'll make sure Curtis stays in at night."

The women finished assembling the bedding, and after checking the radio frequencies, Nash, Gary, Delta and Jo exited the common area. Right before they left, Nash helped Jo change the keyless entry combination and gave each of the women the new code.

"I'll walk Gary to his truck," Delta said.

"See you in the morning." Gary gave them a wave and followed Delta across the driveway.

Jo waited until Nash and she reached the workshop before speaking. "I didn't want to say anything in front of the women, but I'm guessing you have a gun or two on hand if they call for help."

"I do," Nash nodded. "You mentioned your brother, Miles, earlier. How did your conversation with him go?"

"Okay. I told him I accepted his apology and…" Jo's voice trailed off.

"And?"

"He asked if I would reconsider the stipulation of him leaving the area. Miles seems determined to move forward with the purchase of the theater."

"Which might be tied up for a while now that Cantwell is dead," Nash said.

"I pointed out the same thing."

"What are you going to do?"

"I don't know. There's something about the whole thing that's making me uneasy." Jo shoved her hands in her pockets.

"You don't trust him," Nash said.

"Not completely. He's done a complete about-face. Maybe it's because he's anxious to get his hands on the settlement money."

"Money can be a major motivator." Nash nodded toward the common area. "As far as Tara is concerned, it does seem an eerie coincidence she leaves, and this woman – a friend – manages to escape."

"It does," Jo rubbed the back of her neck.

"There's something else," Nash guessed.

"Raylene told me Tara was snooping around in my past before she left."

"Which means?"

"She believes I have money."

"Like money buried in mason jars in the backyard?" Nash joked.

"It's funny, but it's not," Jo shivered. "If the woman was motivated enough to set her home on fire and kill her husband, what's to stop her from targeting me...targeting us?"

Nash sobered as he reached for Jo's hand. "I didn't mean to make light of something so serious. I'll sleep with one eye open and the walkie-talkie next to my bed."

"Thanks, Nash." Jo smiled gratefully. "I don't know what I would do without you."

He pulled Jo into his arms, and she closed her eyes as she placed her head on his chest. "I could stay here forever."

Nash tilted her chin and lowered his head, his soft lips gently touching hers. Jo held her breath, feeling lightheaded by the intensity of her emotions.

The kiss lasted for a long moment until Nash reluctantly pulled away. "Many more kisses like that, and we'll have to elope."

"Wouldn't that set the tongues wagging," Jo laughed.

"We would be the talk of the town."

"As if we aren't already."

Nash released his grip. "Are you going to be okay at the house?"

"We'll be fine. We have Duke, not to mention Delta has a small arsenal of weaponry stashed in her room."

"And you have a handgun in your room?"

Jo nodded. "Loaded and ready to go. Hopefully, I won't need it."

"I saw Delta go back to the house. I'll walk you home." Nash walked Jo to the back door and held it open. "You have my cell phone number. Promise me you'll call if you need anything at all."

"I will." Jo bounced onto her tiptoes and gave Nash a quick kiss. "Be careful."

"Yes, ma'am." He gave Jo's hand a gentle squeeze before turning on his heel and disappearing into the dark night.

Jo checked to make sure she locked the door and climbed the steps to the kitchen. She found Delta rummaging around in the drawers.

"I figured you would be getting ready for bed."

"I was gonna, but first, I gotta find my keys."

"Where did you last have them?"

"I remember putting them on the kitchen table, and now they're gone."

"Which keys are you missing?"

Delta had several sets. She had a master set, including a key to the house, the truck, the women's units and even Jo's SUV. She also had a set for the gun cabinet in her bedroom and a separate set for the cellar's exterior entrance.

"The master keys."

Jo started at the other end of the kitchen and began opening the upper cabinets. "They couldn't have gone far."

The women searched the kitchen, top to bottom. Delta headed to her room to search while Jo went to her office, thinking perhaps her friend had been in there and left them on the desk.

Her next stop was the living room, which is where Delta caught up with her.

"Any luck?" Jo dropped the couch cushion.

"No." Delta spun in a slow circle. "You don't think I took them out to the barn and left them there, do you?"

"We better go look."

"I'll grab a flashlight," Delta said.

"And a gun." Jo circled back through the dining room and waited near the back door. Delta emerged from her room, flashlight in one hand and a small handgun in the other. "I know for certain that I left the keys on the kitchen table."

"It still wouldn't hurt to have a look around. They can't have gone too far."

Delta tightened her grip on the gun, switched the flashlight on and led the way out the back door. "C'mon Duke."

Duke scrambled out of his doggy bed. He flew down the steps and joined the women in the backyard.

"We're going to the barn," Jo told him.

Duke trotted ahead, leading the way while Delta trained the flashlight on the path ahead of them. They had almost reached the barn when the pup let out a loud bark, followed by a low warning growl.

An ominous figure stepped out of the shadows.

Chapter 12

Jo stumbled back, nearly colliding with Delta, who had her weapon poised and pointed.

Nash lunged forward, abruptly stopping when he saw the gun in Delta's hand. "Whoa."

"Good gravy, Nash!" Delta hollered. "What are you doing?"

"What am *I* doing? I thought you two were a couple of prowlers."

"Delta lost her master keys. We're checking the barn."

"I saw a light and came down to investigate." It was then Jo noticed Nash was also holding a gun. "It's a good thing neither one of you decided to shoot first."

"Verify first," Delta said.

Nash relaxed his stance. "Next time you two decide to go wandering around after dark, can you please give me a heads up?"

"I'm sorry. We will," Jo promised. "Now that you're here, you can help us search."

Delta held the flashlight while Nash used Jo's master key to unlock the barn door.

"I wasn't no farther than this room here." Delta headed toward the bin of gifts. Jo began searching the wrapping area while Nash did an interior perimeter check.

Jo finished her search first. "I don't see your keys."

Delta bounced onto the tips of her toes and leaned inside the bin. "I can't for the life of me figure out what happened to them."

"We could check the bakeshop and mercantile," Nash said.

"No. I had them after dinner. I haven't been to either of those places since this morning. I know they're not there."

"We may have to set up a search party in the morning," Jo said.

"Hang on." Delta teetered, half balancing on the edge of the bin, her legs flailing in the air.

Jo reached out to steady her. "What are you doing?"

Delta wiggled her ample bottom back and forth. She inched backward, her feet kicking wildly as she struggled to touch the cement floor. "I got this."

Jo shifted to the side and watched as her friend stumbled backward, triumphantly waving a set of keys in the air. "I found them."

"Awesome," Jo clapped. "Mystery solved. I wonder how they got in the bottom of the bin."

"I don't know. All I know is I have my keys."

"And I'll walk you two back to the house." Nash patted Duke's head. "Good guard dog."

"He definitely gave out a warning," Jo said.

"You might want to keep him downstairs tonight for extra security," Nash suggested.

"I was thinking the same thing," Jo said. "Speaking of security, maybe we should check the surveillance cameras. Perhaps they caught something."

"I already did. There was nothing. They are working. I checked them before I headed upstairs," Nash said. "I'll wait for you to flip the porch light so that I'll know you're inside before heading home."

"I'm sorry we scared you," Delta apologized. "We weren't thinking."

"It's okay. I'll see you in the morning." Nash stood watching until the women were inside the house. Jo flashed the porch lights, and he returned to his apartment.

"The women won't be the only ones who'll be roughing it tonight," Jo said. "I think I'll sleep on the couch."

"I'm sorry about the keys, Jo. I didn't mean to lose them." Delta pressed a hand to her forehead. "I don't know what's wrong with me lately. Do you think I have the onset of Alzheimer's?"

The lost master keys were the most recent incident involving Delta and missing items. It had started a few months back when she'd gone to the store, calling Jo in a panic because she'd forgotten her shopping list and coupons, the two things she never left home without.

Jo had torn the kitchen apart with her friend directing her on where to look. Ten minutes into the search, a sheepish Delta told her she found the list tucked in the side of her purse.

There were other incidents. Delta forgot to shut the oven off, forgot to turn the dishwasher on.

"I..." Jo chose her words carefully. "It does seem you're having more incidents of forgetfulness lately."

"This one and the oven incident are downright scary. Maybe I shouldn't be keeping master keys if I can't keep track of them."

Jo patted her arm. "We have a lot going on. I say cut yourself some slack. If the forgetfulness continues, maybe you should schedule a doctor's appointment. For now, I think it's time to hit the hay."

"Do you need help setting up your bed?"

"I can handle it. Go get some rest. I think we're going to need it." Jo changed into her pajamas before setting up the living room sofa as her makeshift bed.

Duke settled in on the rug nearby while Jo tossed her bathrobe on the end of the couch and slipped under the covers. She tucked the blankets under her chin and lay there, staring at the ceiling for a long time, waiting for her mind to settle.

She said her prayers and a final one that God would lead her regarding Miles's request to stay in Divine.

It was a restless night, and Jo woke early to morning sunlight streaming in through a slit in the living room curtains. Duke stirred as soon as he saw Jo move. He let out a low whine.

"I hear you." Jo threw her covers off. "You want to go out." She shoved her feet into her slippers and traipsed to the door.

After finishing, they tiptoed into the kitchen. Jo filled Duke's food and water dish and then started a pot of coffee before settling in at the kitchen table. She was still there when Delta found her a short time later. "Another rough night?"

"How can you tell?"

"You look like you were run over by a train."

"I feel like it." Jo stifled a yawn. "The couch is comfy for lounging but miserable for sleeping."

"I imagine so. Before the day gets crazy, I've been meaning to ask you for a special recipe, something I can sell in the bakeshop for the holiday season." Delta poured coffee and joined Jo at the kitchen table.

"I have one. It's a recipe for my mom's chocolate macaroons."

"I love me a good macaroon."

"I'll go hunt it down in a few minutes." Jo sipped her coffee, eyeing her friend over the rim of the cup. "You don't look as if you had the best night's sleep, either."

"I spent half of it wide awake, trying to figure out how my keys got into the bottom of the bin. It's driving me crazy."

"Like I said last night, it's been hectic around here lately, and maybe it was nothing more than a memory lapse. Or, they could've fallen out of your pocket, and you didn't notice." Jo wandered over to the kitchen counter. "I'll go see if I can track down the recipe."

"I don't want it to be too much trouble," Delta said. "I figured it would be nice to share a little something special of yours with others."

"It's no trouble." Jo carried her cup into the office and began digging through her files, searching for the worn recipe card her mother had used for years.

She found it mixed in with some legal papers. Her breath caught in her throat as she gazed at the well-worn recipe, the rabbit-ear edges marred with smudges of decades-old chocolate. She ran a light hand over her mother's carefully handwritten words as sudden tears filled her eyes.

Jessica Carlton loved Christmas. She went all out decorating their stately home with not one, but three Christmas trees. The first one greeted friends and family when they entered the grand foyer.

The second, the largest of the three, was placed in front of the bay window in the formal living room. The final tree, Jo's favorite, was placed in the family room, next to the fireplace. The tree was lovingly decorated with treasures Jessica's only child had created.

The decorations were in a box in the back of Jo's bedroom closet. She hadn't taken them out, hadn't looked at them in years. The recipe blurred as her eyes filled with tears.

Jo blinked rapidly. Maybe she was tired. The stress of Tara's unexpected departure, not to mention Miles's request, was weighing heavy on her mind.

She swallowed hard and swiped at her eyes. "Stop this," she sternly scolded herself. "Now is not the time to fall apart."

Jo made a photocopy of the recipe and carefully placed the original back inside the folder before returning to the kitchen. "This is it."

"I'm sure these will be a big hit." Delta gave Jo a hard look as she took the recipe from her friend's outstretched hand. "Are you okay?"

"I'm fine. Just thinking about my parents and how much I miss them. My mother loved Christmas." Jo smiled sadly.

"And you'll always have those wonderful memories, but there are many more memories to make."

"Yes, there are." Jo snaked her hand around to her back and gave a pained look. "The next time I get the bright idea to sleep on the couch, please remind me I'm too old for sofa sleeping."

"You run along and take a nice hot shower to relax those muscles."

Jo made her way upstairs to her bathroom. She took a long leisurely shower, thinking about how her mother would've loved the farm, would've loved the massive fieldstone fireplace, a roaring fire and the handmade stockings lining the mantle.

Jessica would've also loved the idea of a Santa's workshop. A lone tear escaped, trickling down her cheek and mingling with the shower water.

Determined to focus on her blessings, Jo pushed the sad thoughts from her mind and shut the water off. Since the day would be another work-around-the-farm day, she pulled on a pair of old sweatpants and a t-shirt.

She finger-fluffed her hair before trekking down the long hall. Jo started down the stairs when she spied the spiral staircase leading to the widow's walk. It had been weeks since she'd been up there, taking down the cobwebs and sweeping the floor.

Jo climbed the staircase, eased the door open and wandered to the railing. The morning air was crisp and clear, and she could see empty farm fields for miles in every direction.

She admired the view for a moment, basking in the serenity of farm life. Jo turned to go when she spotted a vehicle pulling into the drive. It was the

Smith County sheriff. She watched the vehicle park near the front steps. "Now what?"

Jo hurriedly exited the widow's walk, reaching the front door at the same time Sheriff Franklin did. "Good morning, Sheriff Franklin."

"Good morning Ms. Pepperdine. I'm sorry to bother you again this early but wondered if I could have a few minutes of your time."

"Of course." Jo swung the door open and motioned for him to come inside. "Would you like a cup of coffee?"

"I suppose since I'm making this a regular occurrence, I might as well stay for a cup. If it's not too much trouble."

"Not at all." Jo led him into the kitchen. "Please, have a seat."

"Thank you." The sheriff looked uncomfortable as he eased into the chair near the door.

"I'm guessing this isn't a social visit since you're in uniform." Jo set the coffee on the table and settled into the chair across from him.

"No, ma'am. It's not."

"Then why are you here?" Jo asked bluntly.

"To see what you know about this." The sheriff removed a sheet of paper from his front pocket and handed it to her.

Chapter 13

"This looks like some sort of lawsuit." Jo squinted her eyes and studied the paper. "Someone is suing Divine Bakeshop?"

"Keep reading," the sheriff said grimly.

Jo's eyes scanned the paper. Her heart plummeted when she caught a glimpse of the complainant. "Harrison Cantwell was suing me for food poisoning."

"It appears so. This is the first you've heard of it?"

"He mentioned something the other day at our DABO meeting about getting sick after eating food from the bakeshop." Jo set the paper on the table. "Where did you get this?"

"We found it on his office desk. Self-inflicted gunshot wound has been ruled out as a cause of death. You're certain you knew nothing about this?" the sheriff probed.

"No." The chair scraped loudly on the linoleum floor as Jo abruptly stood. "This is absurd. I've never heard a single customer complain about our baked goods."

"The paper was never filed. Could be Harrison planned to hammer out some sort of settlement with you before moving forward with legal proceedings."

"He would have had to stand in line," Jo mumbled under her breath.

"I'm sorry..."

"It's nothing. Harrison, whom I never even met before the meeting the other day, decides he's going to sue me for food poisoning. He never got around to filing the documents, and now he's dead."

The sheriff leaned back in his chair. "I would like for you to come down to the station for additional questioning."

"And if I refuse?"

"You can, of course, although I don't recommend it."

"What about Carrie Ford? She had some sort of dirt on Harrison."

"We've already questioned Carrie. She's deeply disturbed by the death."

"Meaning, she's too upset to talk."

"Possibly," the sheriff admitted. "I'm not here to talk about her."

"You're here to see me because I appear to have plenty of motive to take Harrison out."

Delta drifted into the kitchen. "I thought I heard voices. A visit from our top cop first thing in the morning can't be a good sign."

"It's not." Jo snatched the paper off the table and handed it to her. "Check this out."

Delta scanned the sheet and made a grunting noise. "He was a jerk. My baked goods never made anyone sick. He probably caught wind Jo had some money and decided to sue."

"I would have to say I agree with you," the sheriff said. "Unfortunately, I still have to question Jo, and I would prefer to do it at the station in the presence of the lead investigator."

"Can I meet you there?" Jo thought about how it would look to the residents if she were placed in the back of a patrol car.

"Yes. Of course. I'm not arresting you." Sheriff Franklin downed the last of his coffee and stood. "How long do you think you'll be?"

"I'll be there within the hour," Jo waited for Delta to walk the sheriff to the door and return to the kitchen. "This is a setup."

"A Miles Parker setup," Delta said. "I ought to go right down there to the theater and give that loser a piece of my mind."

"There's also Carrie Ford. According to Nash, she couldn't stand Harrison Cantwell."

"You're right." Delta snapped her fingers. "Carrie and Harrison got into it at a local bar. She slashed his tires in the parking lot after confronting him. He followed her home. Abner, Carrie's husband at the time, ended up calling the cops, and Harrison was charged with assault and trespassing."

"At the meeting the other day, she made an interesting comment directed at him. I got the impression she has...had some dirt on Harrison."

"Maybe we should pay a visit to Carrie," Delta said.

"I was thinking the same thing. Before we do that, I have to run down to the sheriff's station for my interrogation."

"I'll go with you." Delta grabbed her purse. "Let's tackle one problem at a time. First, we go in for your questioning. After that, we pay a visit to your long-lost half-brother and then Carrie."

Jo climbed into the SUV and Delta darted to the passenger side. "I figured once we track down Miles, we can stop by the deli to see what Marlee has heard."

"We might as well make the rounds and hit up Claire and the Maltons, as well."

They reached the sheriff's station. Delta waited in the reception area while a uniformed officer led Jo to a room in the back. The sheriff and another man Jo had never met before joined her a short time later.

"Would you care for coffee or water, Ms. Pepperdine?" the sheriff asked.

"No, I'm fine. I would like to get this over with as quickly as possible."

"Of course." The sheriff introduced the man. "This is Detective Vine. We're working together on Harrison Cantwell's murder."

"Hello, Ms. Pepperdine. Thank you for coming in. Can you tell me your exact whereabouts on Friday evening and early Saturday morning?"

"I was home. The farm's residents, Nash Greyson, Delta Childress, along with my gardener, Gary Stein, and I spent the evening decorating our Christmas tree."

"All night?" the detective lifted a brow.

"For part of the evening. I went to bed around eleven. Early the next morning, Sheriff Franklin showed up on my doorstep to talk to one of my residents."

The detective consulted his notes. "Tara Cloyne."

"Correct. Unfortunately, Ms. Cloyne left and hasn't returned."

"Do you believe she met with foul play?"

"No, I do not. She was on probation. She took off. In fact, she left a message on my cell phone recently apologizing. I believe she may be on her way to Chicago."

"How well did you know Mr. Cantwell?"

"I met him once, only hours before his death. He attended a Divine Area Business Owner's meeting at the Divine Delicatessen."

"And you had words?"

"You could call it that." Jo shrugged. "He accused me of health department violations at my bakeshop."

"Were you aware he was in the process of filing a lawsuit against your business?"

"Not until this morning," Jo answered truthfully. "For the record, it was a false claim. I believe he planned to try to get some money out of me so I would avoid a lawsuit."

"We found a journal. Cantwell visited your establishment several times with notes about what he purchased and consumed," the sheriff said. "In your opinion, do you think it would be hard to prove your food poisoned him?"

"All I know is I did not kill Harrison Cantwell. I had no knowledge of impending litigation, and I have nothing to hide."

The detective asked a few more leading questions about Jo's whereabouts, her concern over publicity about a possible food poisoning claim and then they were finished.

"You're free to go, Ms. Pepperdine."

Jo slid out of the chair. "I'm sure you have other persons of interest besides me."

"We're speaking to several others," the detective acknowledged. "Thank you for your time."

Jo was silent as she followed the sheriff out of the room. She joined Delta, who was waiting in the lobby. "Well?"

"I think they believe I'm responsible for Cantwell's death. I had a motive. I had the opportunity. I have no witnesses to my whereabouts late Friday night and early Saturday morning."

"I'm putting my money on that sneaky brother of yours. Maybe he and Cantwell concocted a scheme to sue you."

"It's possible." Jo rubbed her eyes. "I guess we better head to town. There has to be more potential suspects than me."

"Carrie and your brother."

"Among others." It was a quick trip to town. Jo parked in front of Marlee's deli and waited for Delta on the sidewalk before they made their way inside.

"Great." Jo frowned at the packed restaurant. "This place is packed."

"We might as well join them," Delta said. "I'm starving."

"I am too. Apparently, police interrogations make me hungry."

"Don't you worry. We're gonna get to the bottom of this." Delta zigzagged past several tables until she found a table for two in the center of the restaurant. "This okay?"

"It's fine." Jo dropped her purse on the table. "I can't believe the man is dead, and now I'm on the hook."

"Not for long. Someone, somewhere around here, has to know something."

One of the servers hustled over. "Hey, Delta, Jo."

"Good morning, Brenda," Jo said. "Is Marlee in this morning?"

"She's in the back. Would you like to see a menu?"

"What's the special?" Delta asked.

"Two eggs any way, your choice of sausage patties or bacon, hash browns and toast."

"I'll take it. Make my eggs over easy with a side of bacon," Delta said.

"Make that two."

"You two are too easy." Brenda finished pouring Delta's coffee. "I'll let Marlee know you're here."

Jo thanked the woman and waited for her to check on another table. "I thought of something. The other day, Sherry told me Harrison Cantwell met with a man here at the deli. They sat in the corner and were talking about an investigation."

"You?" Delta asked.

"Possibly."

Marlee emerged from the back and made her way over. "Hey, gals. What brings you to my neck of the woods?"

"Harrison Cantwell," Jo said. "I just left the sheriff's station after being interrogated."

"They think you had something to do with Cantwell's death?"

"He was in the process of suing me for food poisoning."

"Food poisoning?" Marlee gasped. "That's crazy."

"Apparently, he visited the bakeshop multiple times. He kept notes on when and what he ate and then began working on a claim the bakeshop gave him food poisoning," Jo said.

"That makes no sense. Why would you keep returning to a spot you thought was serving you bad food?"

"That, my friend, is the million-dollar question," Jo said. "My guess is he caught wind I had money. He visited my bakeshop with the sole intent of setting me up for a food poisoning claim. From what I can piece together, his plan was to threaten to sue me in hopes of me paying him off to keep quiet."

"That man." Marlee shook her head. "I wonder if the authorities searched Cantwell's secret stash."

"Miles made a similar comment. What secret stash?"

"Well, I don't know if it was a stash. There's a secret door on the back of his building. I caught him coming out of it one afternoon. He nearly freaked out when he realized I was watching him."

Jo eyed her friend with interest. "What did he do?"

"He started yelling at me, so I left."

"Any idea what's in there?" Delta asked.

"Nope." Marlee shook her head. "Not a clue. Whatever it is, Cantwell definitely wasn't happy I saw him."

Jo tapped Delta's arm. "We need to check it out before we leave town."

"I was thinking." Marlee leaned in and lowered her voice. "Your brother, Miles, was chummy with Cantwell. He even had access to the theater. Maybe he was setting you up."

"I already thought about that. We plan to pay him a visit. There's one more thing." Jo told Marlee about what Sherry had said, how Harrison and another man had visited the deli. They sat in the corner, and Sherry overheard snippets of their conversation. "She heard one of them say something about an investigation. I wondered if perhaps you had noticed them too."

Marlee shifted her feet as she stared at Jo thoughtfully. "You know, now that you mention it, I did see Cantwell in here the other night with another man. I don't know who he was."

"Oh." Jo's face fell. "He was one of the last people to see Cantwell alive. The fact he mentioned some sort of investigation might be a clue. Sherry said they didn't look very happy."

"Wait a minute." Marlee pressed the palms of her hands together. "You know what? I think I may be able to figure out who he was."

Chapter 14

"Give me a minute." Marlee strode to the back of the restaurant and out of sight.

During the wait, Brenda delivered their breakfast. They were halfway through with their food when Marlee returned, triumphantly waving a slip of paper in the air. "Sherry is sharp as a tack. She remembered what Harrison and the mystery man ordered, which helped me find their receipt."

"Who was it?" Jo asked.

"He met with Charles Stripling. Stripling paid for dinner. I figured I had a decent shot at tracking it down. Harrison was so cheap; I was sure he hadn't been the one to pick up the tab."

"Who is Charles Stripling?"

"Not *who* but *what*," Marlee said.

"He's the biggest ambulance chaser in all of Kansas," Delta answered.

"An attorney."

"A slimy, grimy, first-rate, sue-your-grandmother-for-a-buck attorney," Marlee said.

"Cantwell was working with Stripling to sue me." Jo felt as if someone had punched her in the gut.

"That would be my guess."

Jo leaned back in the chair and closed her eyes. "This doesn't look good."

"Cantwell planned to blindside you with a claim of food poisoning, probably hoping you would offer to settle in exchange for him not filing the claim."

"And if I didn't, he was going to hire this high-profile attorney to sue me," Jo said. "Which means this makes me even more suspect. They might as well throw the cuffs on."

"Not so fast," Delta shook her head. "You're not a quitter, Joanna Pepperdine. Someone took Cantwell out, and it wasn't you."

"I'm with Delta," Marlee said. "I'll keep my ear to the ground. Everyone is talking about the death. It's only a matter of time before his killer slips up. Maybe you should pop your sleuthing hat on and get to work."

"You're right. I guess I never figured someone would have the nerve to try to blackmail me."

"There are a lot of bad people out there," Delta said. "Look at Harrison, God rest his soul. Speaking of Harrison, we're gonna go look for his secret storage area next."

Marlee returned to the kitchen while the women finished their food. Jo flagged Brenda down to settle the bill. She handed her a twenty and a ten. "Keep the change."

"Thanks, Ms. Pepperdine."

"Jo," Jo smiled.

"Jo." Brenda shoved the cash and bill copy in her apron pocket. "I heard that you're hosting a Christmas party for Spirit of the Season. My sister's son is in the program this year." She told them her brother-in-law skipped town with another woman, leaving her sister and nephew without any financial support. "She moved in with my mother, but money is tight."

"I'm sorry to hear that."

"I wasn't telling you to make you feel bad." Brenda reached for the stack of dirty dishes. "I said it so you would know you're helping real people, and I think the Santa workshop sounds awesome. When Trevor, my nephew, found out he was visiting Santa, he was bouncing off the walls."

"I can't wait to meet him."

Delta watched Brenda finish stacking the dirty plates and walk away. "You see that? People like Cantwell are bent on doing bad things while you're always helping others."

"I try."

"God don't take lightly to those hurting others. That's why I'm certain we're going to get to the bottom of what happened."

"I hope so."

After exiting the restaurant, the women crossed to the other side of the street, stopping when they reached the entrance to the old theater. Jo tugged on the door handles. The doors were locked. "We'll try around back."

They walked to the end of the block, circling around to the rear of the building and a small storage unit. "This must be the storage unit the authorities searched the other day."

Delta studied the exterior. "Not much to look at." She turned her attention to the back of the theater, running a light hand over the red bricks. "Finding a secret door might be tricky."

"We're already here. We might as well try. I'll start at this end." Jo made a beeline for the corner closest to the street.

"I'll start at the other end." Delta walked to the other side and began making her way toward Jo and the center of the building. "I think I found something." She waited for her friend to join her. "There's a small crack. See it? It makes a perfect outline."

"It does." Jo took a step back. "Yes. I definitely see it."

Delta placed the palms of her hands on the bricks and pressed lightly. "Maybe it's a settling crack."

"But Marlee said she saw a door." Jo bounced on her tiptoes and traced the crack with her finger. "There has to be some sort of trick to opening it."

She knelt on the ground, running her fingers along the bottom of the crack. Jo reached the halfway point when her fingers touched cold metal. "I think I may have found something."

Delta dropped to her knees.

"There's some sort of lever." Jo pressed on the metal piece. Nothing happened.

"Let me try."

Jo scooted to the side to make room for Delta. She slid her fingers into the crevice. 'I can't quite..."

"We need light." Jo removed her cell phone from her pocket and switched it on before lowering onto the ground. She beamed the light into the small opening. "The lever must be spring loaded."

"I might have something in my purse long enough to trigger it." Delta reached inside and pulled out a pair of clippers. "What about these?"

"It's worth a try." Jo extended the handle and jabbed it into the opening. "It's too short. I need something longer."

"Let me see..." Delta opened her purse's side pocket. "This might do the trick." She handed Jo a dull knife.

"You carry a butter knife in your purse?"

"It's a heating knife."

"A heating knife?" Jo turned it over in her hand.

"To melt butter."

"Now I've seen it all," Jo teased.

Delta made an unhappy noise. "Don't judge."

"I'm not." Jo chuckled and then returned to the task of jimmying the lever. She wedged it into the opening and pressed as hard as she could. "I...think I've got it."

Ting. The lever released, and the door popped open.

"Awesome." Jo placed both hands on the bottom of the door and gently pulled. The door groaned in protest, swinging partly open before abruptly stopping. "It doesn't wanna open."

"Let me try." Jo stepped out of the way and watched as Delta kicked it with her foot.

"Be careful," Jo warned. "Harrison probably has it booby-trapped."

"I think it's rusted shut." Delta peered into the opening. "I can't see a thing."

"Cell phone to the rescue." Jo beamed the bright light inside the dark space. "No way. You're not going to believe this."

Chapter 15

The secret room was full of toys...boxes of toys, bicycles, basketball hoops, soccer balls, stuffed animals, dolls and board games filled every square inch of the cramped space. "Are you thinking what I'm thinking?"

"Harrison Cantwell was the one who stole the children's toys."

Jo switched her cell phone from flashlight to camera and snapped several pictures. "I'm sending these to Pastor Murphy to see if he's able to identify them."

Delta waited quietly until Jo finished sending the photos. "What on earth would possess him to steal toys from children in need?"

"I don't know."

The pastor was quick to reply, asking where she had found the toys.

"He wants to know where I found them," Jo said. "He's on his way down here."

"Should we contact Sheriff Franklin?" Delta asked.

"Let's have the pastor confirm they're his first."

"Because the sheriff is gonna want to know what we were doing back here."

"Exactly, and there's no sense in inviting trouble unless we have to."

It didn't take long for the pastor to arrive. Jo was the first to see him hurrying down the alley. "How did you find this?"

"We were having breakfast at Marlee's deli. She mentioned how she once caught a glimpse of a secret door. Delta and I figured we might as well check it out. We got to looking around and noticed a hairline crack in the bricks. I found a small lever and Voila!" Jo snapped her fingers. "We found a secret storage room. Check it out."

She turned her cell phone's light on and handed it to him. "You'll need this."

The pastor stepped in front of the door. "I...I'm almost certain these are the toys that were stolen. There was one very special gift. Let me see if I can find it."

The light dimmed as Pastor Murphy crept into the room. There was a dull *thud*. He emerged, triumphantly waving a small box. "This is it."

"What is it?"

"It's a planting gift. They're starter seeds. One of the children has cancer and requested a magical growing garden."

"There's no doubt these are your toys," Delta said.

"None at all." The pastor shook his head.

"I guess it's time to call the sheriff." Jo dialed his number and left a brief message, asking him to meet her behind the old theater.

While they waited, the women watched the pastor excitedly sort through the piles. "I can't believe it. They're all here. At least I think all of the toys are here. Why would Harrison steal children's toys?"

"He wasn't a nice person. That's an excellent question and one that might never get answered." The sound of tires crunching on gravel echoed in the alley. Jo caught a glimpse of the front of a patrol car. "He's here."

The trio waited for the sheriff to exit his vehicle and join them.

"Hello, ladies, pastor. What have you got?"

"This." Jo motioned toward the open doorway.

The sheriff stepped past them and made his way inside. He emerged a short time later. "How did you find this? We searched every square inch of this place."

"Delta and I were in the deli this morning, talking to Marlee. She remembered catching a glimpse of a secret door. After Delta and I left, we decided to see if we could find it." Jo eased the door shut. "We noticed a crack in the bricks. I followed the crack to the bottom and ran my hand along the edge. That's when I found the lever that opened the door."

The sheriff turned to Pastor Murphy. "Are you able to identify the toys?"

"I sure can. These are mine."

"Let me go grab my paperwork. You may have to wait a day or so to claim the items."

"I can wait two days," the pastor said excitedly.

When Sheriff Franklin returned, he was holding a clipboard. "Technically, this might be considered as evidence in a crime. That's the reason I can't let you take the items with you." He removed a pen.

"Give me a day or so to run this through the proper channels, and then it should be clear for you to claim your property."

The pastor pumped the sheriff's hand. "Thank you so much. You don't know what a miracle this is." He turned to Jo and squeezed her hand. "Thank you, Jo and Delta. I don't know how I can ever repay you. First the check, then Santa's workshop and now this."

"You're welcome," Jo began following the pastor out of the alley.

"Hang on there, ladies." The sheriff stopped them. "Are there any more secret rooms you're itching to explore?"

"No." Jo shook her head. "If we hear about any, we'll be sure to let you know."

The women returned to the front of the building and Main Street, leaving the sheriff standing in the doorway, scratching his head.

"I wonder if Miles knows about the secret room," Delta said.

"He mentioned Cantwell talking about a secret stash but didn't elaborate." Jo studied the front of the theater. "I suppose he could be back at the motel where he's staying."

"Since we're already here, let's chat with Claire and the Maltons," Delta suggested.

The women found Claire working at the laundromat. She caught Jo's eye as they stepped inside. "Speak of the devil...or should I say, angel."

"Were you talking about us?" Jo asked.

"I sure was. A detective was here snooping around a few minutes ago, asking a lot of questions about you, the bakeshop and your brother."

"He was asking about Miles?"

"Yeah. I got the impression..." Claire's voice drifted off.

"What impression?" Delta asked.

"I think he was trying to link Jo and her brother to Cantwell's death."

"That makes sense," Jo said. "He probably thinks since Cantwell was in the process of suing me, I enlisted the help of my brother, who was working with Cantwell, to take him out."

"Suing?" Claire's mouth dropped open. "Cantwell was suing you?"

"It's a long story," Jo sighed. "Let's just say I'm a prime suspect and with what you said, more than likely at the top of the list. I should probably go ahead and give my attorney, Chris, a call and let him know what's going on."

Delta leaned an elbow on the counter. "We're trying to figure out who had the most motive and opportunity to take Cantwell out."

"Half the town," Claire said. "If you recall, he threatened to report me to the county. He was telling Wayne Malton he was late on his rent. He was complaining about your baked goods and threatening to call the health department. I'm sure he had Marlee on the hook for something too."

"Not to mention Carrie Ford," Jo said. "He was also the one who stole the kids' Christmas gifts from the church."

"Harrison Cantwell stole the kids' toys?" Claire's jaw dropped.

"Delta and I found them in a secret storage area behind the theater."

"I can't believe it."

"That's not all. We found out Cantwell met with Charles Stripling, a well-known ambulance-chasing attorney from Kansas City."

"He is," Claire agreed, "His face is plastered on highway billboards from here to Texas. Why was Cantwell meeting with that snake?"

"I believe they were working on filing a lawsuit against me for food poisoning." Jo briefly explained to Claire about the litigation the investigators found on Cantwell's desk. "Marlee discovered Cantwell and Stripling met at her restaurant only hours before his death."

"If you took that man out, I think they should give you some sort of award."

"Claire," Jo chided.

"Well, he was a mean-spirited, evil man." Frustrated, Claire slapped her palm on the counter. "It just isn't fair. Rumor around town is he died from a single gunshot wound. Maybe he killed himself. I think they should call it a suicide and let us all rest in peace."

"But more than likely someone took him out, which leaves a killer roaming the streets," Jo pointed out.

Claire straightened her back. "If someone is responsible for his death, they're bound to slip up and start talking."

"We can only hope."

Delta and Jo wandered out of the laundromat and across the street to Tool Time Hardware. "Wayne's usually in the back." Jo headed to the checkout counter. "Is Wayne or Charlotte around?"

The man shook his head. "They're both off this afternoon. They won't be back until tomorrow morning."

Jo thanked the man, and they returned to the SUV.

Delta hopped in the passenger seat and waited for Jo to join her. "Now what?"

"I think it's time to pay Miles a surprise visit. I'm sure the investigators have already talked to him, but it wouldn't hurt to have a word with him myself. He mentioned he was staying at a motel outside of town."

"There's only one. It's Centerpoint Motor Lodge. I'll tell you how to get there." Delta directed Jo out of town and toward the area's top tourist attraction – the contiguous center of the United States.

They reached the main road leading to the spot and were almost there when Delta told Jo to turn off.

She steered onto a paved driveway, past a small sign, *Centerpoint Motor Lodge*, through a tunnel of trees and into a parking lot.

"I've never noticed this place before." Jo eased into an empty parking spot.

"It's a hidden gem," Delta said. "It's been around for as long as I can remember. In its heyday, you had to book this place months in advance to get a room."

"It's not busy now." Jo wrinkled her nose and peered through the windshield at the empty parking lot and nondescript brown brick building.

"They done good 'til the interstate came along, and all of the businesses moved closer to the highway." Delta joined Jo in front of the vehicle. "Sad to say, but a lot of the mom and pop places have fallen to the wayside."

"I'm surprised this one managed to survive."

"That's because of the Divine Fall Festival, not to mention the fact it's right next to the area's main tourist attraction." Delta, along with Jo, passed by the blinking neon "vacancy" sign and made their way inside.

The motel's lobby floor sported worn brown tiles, the exact same color as the exterior. There was a vending machine in the corner of the lobby with a display of pamphlets touting the nearby tourist attractions next to it.

The lingering aroma of mothballs and floor wax reminded Jo of her grandmother's house.

Delta lightly tapped the silver bell on top of the counter.

The door on the opposite end opened, and a young woman emerged. "Can I help you?"

"Yes," Jo hesitantly smiled. "We're looking for a friend, Miles Parker. I believe he's staying here."

"Mr. Parker." The woman lowered her gaze and studied the computer screen. "I'm sorry, but he isn't here."

"I didn't see his car, so I figured he may have gone somewhere," Jo said.

"No." The woman shook her head. "He checked out early this morning."

Chapter 16

"Checked out?"

"Yes, ma'am. I remember him. He was here first thing this morning saying something came up and he asked for a refund."

"Did he say where he was headed?" Delta asked.

"Nope." The woman shook her head. "Now that I think about it, he seemed kinda nervous. He kept looking at his watch."

Delta and Jo exchanged a quick glance.

"Thank you for your time." Jo was the first to exit the motel office and waited for Delta to join her on the sidewalk. "What do you think?"

"I think Miles Parker murdered Harrison Cantwell. Maybe he figured the investigators were onto him, and he took off."

"He'll never get his money from me if he's on the run," Jo said.

"Then, he shoulda thought about that before he took another man's life."

Jo mulled over the new information as they pulled out of the parking lot. "What if the authorities think I took a hit out on Harrison after discovering he planned to sue me? I hired my brother to do the deed, and now Miles, with the heat on him, took off."

"I reckon that's a possibility." Delta tugged on her seatbelt. "But I would think the investigators would know a fine, upstanding citizen like yourself was not involved in the man's death. In fact, almost everyone in town knows you and Miles were at odds."

"Until recently." Jo tightened her grip on the steering wheel. "This is terrible. Maybe Miles knew the authorities were taking a closer look at me and decided to leave, heaping even more suspicion on me."

226

"I told you from the get-go I didn't trust the man. This just confirms my suspicions."

The women discussed Miles's sudden departure until they reached the farm. By the time Jo pulled into the drive it was late morning, and she realized she hadn't checked in with the women or Nash.

So much had happened in a few short hours, from the sheriff's arrival and producing the paperwork for possible litigation, finding out Harrison had contacted a well-known attorney, discovering the stash of stolen toys and last, but not least, Miles's abrupt departure, that it left her head spinning.

Jo reached for the door handle, and Delta stopped her. "I can see your wheels spinning over what's happened today."

"I...can't believe it. A week ago, I didn't even know who Harrison Cantwell was, and now I'm a suspect in his death."

"God has a way of turning the worst of situations into the best," Delta said. "Who knows the reasons why."

"I'm gonna run next door and make sure nothing else happened last night." Jo slid out of the driver's seat. "Crud. We forgot about stopping by Carrie Ford's place."

"You're right. We're gonna have to try to squeeze it in later. For now, I best get to the kitchen and start thinking about lunch and dinner."

The women parted ways with Jo stopping by the mercantile where Kelli and Michelle were working.

Michelle noticed Jo first, and she darted across the room. "Hey, Jo."

"Hello, Michelle. I'm sorry I didn't check in earlier. Delta and I had a minor emergency pop up, and we drove into town. How did everything go last night?"

"There was no sign of anyone near the women's area. Nash was here earlier, asking about flannel shirts. I'm not sure why. Other than that, it's been quiet."

Jo thanked her for the update. She exited the mercantile and crossed over to the bakeshop, where Raylene was arranging a tray of reindeer cupcakes and snowman sugar cookies. "Those look tasty."

"They are. Would you like to try one?"

Jo shook her head. "Delta and I ate breakfast at Marlee's place, and I'm still full. I spoke to Michelle. She said things were quiet around here last night."

"They were," Raylene agreed. "Any word on Harrison Cantwell's death?"

"You have no idea." Jo briefly closed her eyes. "It's a mess."

"I'm sorry to hear that."

A customer approached the display case, and Jo wandered out of the store. The overhead door to Nash's workshop was open. The sound of a grinder echoed loudly.

She spied Nash and Gary standing side by side in front of the workbench, working on what appeared to be a reindeer.

Jo waited for the grinder to stop and the men to notice her.

"Hey, Jo." Nash removed his safety goggles and set them on the tabletop.

"Hey, guys." Jo joined them. "What a cute reindeer."

"This here is Rudolph." Gary tapped the tip of the reindeer's round nose. "We have Rudolph plus two more. "What do you think of the sleigh?"

"The sleigh?" Jo pivoted. It was then she noticed a large wooden sleigh in the corner. "You're done with it already?"

"Only the frame." Nash followed her to the other side of the room. "We sanded, sealed and assembled it. We're waiting for the glue to dry so Santa can test its sturdiness, and then we'll start painting."

Jo ran a light hand over the curved front board. "It's going to be awesome."

"And completely storable." Nash showed Jo how the sides slid into the slots of the front and rear panels, fitting like the pieces of a large puzzle. "After we're done, we can disassemble it and store it flat for next year."

"I love it," Jo said. "It's perfect. Thank you for helping me follow through with my crazy ideas."

"Gary and I are thrilled to be able to be a part of it," Nash said sincerely. "I saw your SUV was gone first thing this morning. Is everything all right?"

"Not...completely." Jo's eyes slid to Gary, who was sanding an antler.

"We can step outside," Nash suggested.

Jo nodded and followed him out. They wandered to the corner of the workshop, a safe distance from the open door. "Sheriff Franklin was on my doorstep this morning. He found a paper in Harrison Cantwell's office. It was a court filing."

"Harrison was suing someone?" Nash asked. "I'm not surprised."

"He was planning to sue Divine Bakeshop for food poisoning."

A muscle in Nash's jaw twitched. "Which puts you at the top of the list of suspects."

"Yes. And Miles is gone. He checked out of his motel this morning."

"Maybe he planned to leave."

"Not according to the motel clerk. She told Delta and me that he'd had a change of plans, and he seemed nervous. He kept looking at his watch."

Nash rubbed the back of his neck. "Miles has access to Harrison's place. Harrison is in the process of suing you, and his body is found behind the theater."

Jo picked up. "Miles is my half-brother, and now he's gone, leaving me holding the bag. I have no eyewitnesses who can verify my whereabouts around the time Harrison was murdered."

"Do you think Miles murdered Harrison, knowing he was in the process of suing you and set you up?"

"Maybe." Jo shrugged. "There could be a dozen different scenarios. I do know all roads lead back to Miles, who had the opportunity. Maybe his motive was for me to take the fall."

"Then, he shouldn't have taken off. This makes him look suspicious, as well," Nash pointed out. "He won't be collecting on his settlement if he's on the run."

"I thought the same thing." Jo sucked in a breath, wishing more than anything the nightmare would go away. "I talked to the women. They said all was quiet around the farm last night."

"It was for them, but there are some things I need to show you."

"You found something?"

233

"Yes, and so did Gary. I'll let Gary go first."

The couple returned to the workshop. Gary had finished sanding the antlers and was working on one of the reindeer's hooves.

"Hey, Gary. I hate to interrupt because you're really knocking out this sanding business," Nash joked.

"I never realized I enjoyed woodworking this much. I was thinking...I haven't bought Delta's Christmas gift yet." Gary removed his safety glasses. "Do you think Delta would like a hope chest?"

"She might. Or you could build her a gun cabinet," Jo suggested. "She's running out of space in the one she has."

Gary's eyes lit. "A gun case? I like that idea. It would be more up Delta's alley. I think I will. I figure it'll only take me a few days to build it. Do you know what her favorite color is?"

Jo eyed Gary thoughtfully, trying hard to remember if Delta had ever mentioned having a favorite color. "I...don't know. She wears a lot of red."

"Red," Gary repeated. "I can use some of the leftover red paint from the sleigh."

"I'm sure Delta would love a new gun case," Jo patted his arm.

"And I can even monogram it for her," Gary said excitedly.

"I think you should get on it as soon as possible." Nash changed the subject. "I told Jo you noticed something odd this morning when you got here."

Chapter 17

"I did. It's probably best if I show you." Gary picked up a small swatch of green cloth and motioned for Jo to follow him out of the workshop, past the barn and to the gardening shed on the other side.

"I found this piece of cloth." He tapped a sliver of splintered wood on the corner of the shed. "It was hanging right here."

Jo studied the scrap of material. "It looks like a piece of a flannel shirt."

"That's what I was thinking," Nash, who had followed them out, spoke.

"I know it wasn't here before because we searched this place the other day."

"What about the women? Maybe one of them caught their shirt on the corner," Jo theorized.

"Nope," Nash shook his head. "I already checked with each of them."

"Maybe a customer?"

"It could have been someone who visited the bakeshop or mercantile, but what are the chances?" Nash asked.

"Slim to none. This is...disturbing." Jo shifted her gaze to the long stretch of empty road out front. Across the street were acres of farmland. There wasn't a neighbor for miles around, except for Dave Kilwin. The abundance of privacy had been a major selling point and one that appealed to Jo when she first looked at the property.

Could it be whoever had damaged the vending machine was also messing around out front?

"Maybe we should have a look around to see if we can find anything else," Jo said.

"We already did, about an hour ago," Nash said.

"I should probably get back to the workshop. I need to finish working on Vixen's hooves." Gary rounded the corner of the building.

"I also found something on the surveillance cameras, but before I show you, we have one more stop." Nash placed a light hand on Jo's back and led her to the front of the mercantile and bakeshop. "Check it out."

"Check what out?"

"The motion sensor lights I installed in front of the businesses."

Jo shaded her eyes and studied the lights. "They're broken."

"My guess is someone used a sharp object to knock them out."

"So the lights wouldn't go on," Jo whispered.

"Let me show you the surveillance footage." They stepped inside Nash's small office, and he closed the door behind them.

Jo perched on the edge of a stool while Nash took the one beside her. He turned his laptop on and reached for the mouse.

With a couple of clicks, Nash brought up the app for the surveillance cameras. He pressed the play button, and a black screen appeared.

"What am I looking for?"

"You'll see."

Jo grew silent as she focused her attention on the computer. She was almost ready to give up when she caught a white blip dash across the screen.

"Did you catch that?"

"What was it?"

"I'll play it again, this time in slow motion." Nash tapped the keys.

A grainy white shadow floated past the camera. The figure turned away and then slowly faded from sight.

Jo blinked rapidly. "Was that a person?"

"I was hoping you could tell me. You wanna watch it again?"

"Yeah."

Nash played the recording again.

"It almost looks as if it wasn't human."

"Maybe it was one of the angelic beings that protect this place," Nash said.

"It could be one of our guardian angels." Jo straightened her back. "Or perhaps it was a person. If I look at it from a different angle, I could swear I see long hair."

"Either way, something caught the camera's attention."

"I'm going to call Sheriff Franklin to see if he has an update on Tara or the escapee, Karen."

"In the meantime, I'll work on fixing the broken lights."

Jo thanked him and returned to the house. She passed through the kitchen before making her way to her office.

She slumped down in the chair and gazed sightlessly out the window. What had happened to Harrison Cantwell? Had Miles murdered him, knowing the man was in the process of attempting to solicit a cash settlement in exchange for not filing a lawsuit against her bakeshop for food poisoning?

Why Jo? There were dozens of other people Cantwell could have targeted. A disturbing thought occurred to her...unless Cantwell and Miles concocted a scheme to get more money out of Jo – even more than what Miles would be paid in their settlement.

But why would Miles murder Cantwell? He would be a prime suspect, unless – going back to, he knew about Cantwell's potential claim. He'd seemed so sincere in his apology, and Jo had always prided herself on being a good judge of character.

Perhaps she had let her personal feelings cloud her judgment. There was one more sticking point. If Miles was responsible for Cantwell's death and he was betting on her being charged with the man's murder, where was he?

Jo dialed the sheriff's number and left a brief message asking him to call at his earliest convenience. She set the phone on her desk and reached for the most recent version of the settlement agreement.

She kept going back to the stipulation that Miles be allowed to reside anywhere he wanted without restriction, meaning Divine. His goal was to buy the theater. Jo remembered the look of excitement on his face as he shared his vision for it.

Cantwell's death could mean Miles's dream of owning the property would never materialize.

Jo's cell phone chirped, jolting her out of her musings. It was the sheriff. "Hello, Sheriff Franklin. Thank you for calling me back. With everything else going on, I forgot to ask if you had an update on the prison escapee, Karen Griffin."

"As you know, we have a confirmed sighting of Ms. Griffin by your resident. Griffin was also sighted at a local gas station this morning. Unfortunately, by the time we got the call and could get there, she was gone."

"Which means she's still in the area." Jo grabbed an ink pen and began clicking the end. "What about Tara?"

"We've contacted her family in Chicago. They claim they haven't seen or heard from her yet. They promised to let us know if she shows up."

"So both of them could still be in the area," Jo said.

"It's possible. While I have you on the phone, I was wondering if you knew how I might be able to locate your half-brother, Miles Parker. It appears he checked out of his motel, and his current whereabouts are unknown."

"I was looking for him too," Jo said.

"You don't know where he went?"

"No. Not a clue." Jo started to speak and then stopped.

"What were you going to say?"

"I was thinking...Miles and I haven't been on the best of terms. What if he knew about Cantwell's potential litigation against me, he decided to take Cantwell out and have me take the fall."

"I have considered the possibility. We're covering all angles."

Jo shifted the phone to her other ear. "We still believe someone is hanging around the farm." She told him about the piece of cloth Gary found clinging to the side of the gardening shed and how the surveillance cameras had caught a shadowy figure the previous night.

The office door swung open. Delta peeked around the corner, and Jo motioned her inside.

"We've stepped up patrols and will continue to do so until the woman has been apprehended," the sheriff promised.

Jo thanked him and ended the call.

"No news on Tara?" Delta asked after Jo hung up.

"Nope. Nothing. She hasn't shown up at her parent's house. Karen Griffin is still on the run and was spotted at an area gas station. By the time the police arrived, she was gone." Jo told Delta about the piece of fabric, the shadowy figure caught on the surveillance camera and the broken lights.

"What if the woman is hanging around here?"

"I'm beginning to wonder. Even if the shadowy figure was an apparition..."

"Or an angel," Delta interrupted.

"Or one of Divine's guardian angels," Jo said. "Angelic beings wouldn't necessarily leave scraps of clothing behind."

"How are we gonna figure out who's lurking around at night?"

Jo pressed her fingers to her chin. "I need to give it some thought, but before we can try to figure out what's going on around here, we have one more person to pay a visit to."

Chapter 18

"I forgot how bright Carrie's place was." Delta peered through the front windshield at the whimsical cotton candy shutters and bright yellow siding of Carrie Ford's home.

"At least it matches." Jo jabbed her finger in the direction of the building next to the pink garage. She read the sign above the door. "Carrie's Custom Creations."

"I can't imagine the neighbors being too keen on her operating a business in this swanky neighborhood."

"She got away with painting her house like Candyland. They probably gave up." Jo followed her friend into the small building. Two plastic vinyl chairs were near the entrance, and a brown laminate table was between the chairs.

Carrie, who was standing at the counter, turned. Her mouth and face were covered with what reminded Jo of a combination dive mask and a surgical mask.

"Jo. Delta." She snatched a cloth off the table and flung it on top of a nearby object.

"What in the world?" Jo's stomach churned at the pungent pickle smell hanging in the air.

Delta made a gagging noise. "Good grief. What is that disgusting smell?"

"It's formaldehyde. I use it to preserve my creations. Do you want to check out one of my latest projects?" Carrie removed the mask before grabbing Jo's hand and dragging her to the workbench. "Isn't it a beaut?"

Delta flung her arm across her face and stared at the shiny black log hanging from a clothesline. "What is it?"

"You really can't tell?" Carrie looked crestfallen. "It's a bat. See the wings?"

Jo tilted her head. "Yes. Actually, I do see it now."

"A bat?" Delta's eyes widened in horror. "Don't they carry rabies or something?"

"It's dead. This bat isn't going to bite anyone."

"It's still creepy."

"Speaking of creepy," Jo said. "We're here to talk about Harrison Cantwell's death...murder."

"I've already talked to Detective Vine and the sheriff," Carrie slipped a pair of gloves on and reached for the bat. "I told them someone did this town a huge favor by getting rid of that creep."

"I heard there was no love lost between you," Jo said.

"Love lost?" Carrie snorted. "I hate to speak ill of the dead, but he was the biggest jerk who ever walked the face of the earth. I think he's one of the reasons poor Abner died at such a young age. All of that running around, harassing innocent people. It finally came back and bit Harrison Cantwell in the butt."

Jo perked up. "Harassing innocent people like who?"

"Take your pick. Let's start with his tenants...the Maltons, not to mention the owners of Four Corners Mini Mart. He was giving Claire a hard time." Carrie shot Jo a sideways glance. "I heard he was coming after you next."

"He was, which is why I'm at the top of the list of suspects."

"No." Carrie shook her head. "I'm at the top. It was no secret that Harrison and I detested each other. If you're here to ask if I did him in, the answer is no. He wasn't worth a prison sentence. I figured one of these days he would cross the wrong person, and it would be the end of him."

"If you had to guess, who do you think took him out?"

Carrie fiddled with the tip of her glove. "Do you really want to know?"

"Yes," Jo nodded, "I do."

"Pastor Murphy."

Jo's jaw dropped. "Pastor Murphy?"

"Yep," Carrie nodded firmly. "I heard Harrison stole the kids' Christmas gifts. Why do you think he stole them?" She didn't wait for Delta or Jo to reply. "He didn't hate children, although he never cared for them. The real reason was that he hated Pastor Murphy."

Jo struggled to wrap her head around the thought someone would consider the beloved pastor a suspect...or that he had any enemies. "Why?"

"Harrison Cantwell's deceased wife."

"He was married?" Jo asked.

"I remember her," Delta chimed in. "Ellen. She was the sweetest lady. I always wondered how she managed to become shackled to Harrison."

"Money. Ellen grew up dirt poor. Her parents pushed her toward him because his family had money. Of course, as the years went on there was trouble in the marriage. Ellen spent more and more time volunteering at the church, which is when the real trouble began."

"Ellen decided to leave Harrison," Jo guessed.

"Yep. She was in love with Pastor Murphy."

Jo stared blankly, trying to digest the news. "So Harrison Cantwell blamed Pastor Murphy for his wife leaving him."

"One hundred percent. Rumor around town was Pastor Murphy had no idea. He tried to let Ellen down gently, but she took it hard."

"What happened?" Jo asked.

"She committed suicide," Delta answered. "I always figured Harrison drove her to it."

"It could be a combination of Ellen being heartbroken and being desperate to escape

Harrison," Carrie shrugged. "So that's why I think it was Pastor Murphy. Harrison has been harassing him for years, doing whatever he could to make the poor pastor's life miserable. I think he finally snapped."

"How do you know this?" Delta asked suspiciously.

"I was the church's pianist for several years. Rumors go 'round."

"You're right. I plum forgot about that."

Jo began to pace. "Pastor Murphy is passionate about his Spirit of the Season program. Harrison Cantwell waits until he's certain the toys have been purchased, and then he breaks into the church's storage area and steals them. The pastor suspects he's responsible and confronts him. They argue, and the pastor accidentally kills Harrison."

"Have you mentioned your theory to the authorities?" Delta asked.

Carrie picked up a pair of scissors. "And tell them what? Pastor Murphy is a suspect? I'm sure they've already questioned him. Besides, I figure if the pastor murdered Harrison, it was God's will and an accident."

Jo's eyes fell on the white sheet of cloth Carrie had tossed on top of the table. A bright red shoe peeked out from beneath. She reached for the sheet. "What's this?"

"It's a surprise." Carrie dashed across the room, wedging herself between Jo and the table. "You can't look."

"A surprise?" Jo's curiosity was piqued.

"For the children's visit to Santa's workshop. When I found out about it, I wanted to contribute something special. I started working on it the other day."

"Something from your taxidermy business," Delta guessed.

"It's gonna blow your socks off." Carrie clapped her hands. "If I have time, I'll make a set."

"A set of what?" An inkling of dread filled Jo as she eyed the tip of the red shoe.

"You'll have to wait. I was gonna call you to ask if you needed an extra hand for the party."

The look on Carrie's face was so full of hope that Jo didn't have the heart to tell her 'no.' "We can always use extra help. Perhaps you can pass out hot chocolate."

Carrie beamed. "Great. I'll come a little early to help set up." She gently patted the side of the cloth. "You won't be disappointed. My masterpiece will enhance the enjoyment of all."

"I can hardly wait," Delta muttered under her breath.

Carrie ignored the comment. "Now that you're here, I can give you a mini class in taxidermy."

"I don't..."

Carrie cut Jo off. "I know you're super busy and have been trying to find a time to stop by to check it out. Since you're already here, this won't take long. You might be surprised by how much you enjoy learning about Carrie's Custom Creations."

Jo reluctantly followed Carrie to the bat stand. "Benny, here, is a fine specimen. Mrs. Petersen brought him in. I've been working on him in between the Christmas surprise. She's anxious to get him back."

"The woman had a pet bat?"

"Benny showed up right after Mr. Petersen passed away. Joyce believed Benny was a reincarnation of her husband, and he was watching over her."

"That's kooky," Delta shoved a hand on her hip.

"Who am I to judge?" Carrie asked. "We each have our own beliefs about how loved ones reach across the grave to comfort us in our time of need."

"True," Jo said. "The woman grew attached to the bat. He died, and she brought him here so you could work your magic."

"Correct." Carrie nodded. "Benny was an excellent candidate for forever preservation." She explained it was sometimes difficult to determine how long the animal had been deceased.

"You can tell a lot from the eyes. Let's take Benny, for example. His eyes were still perfectly rounded, which means he recently passed. If the eyes have dried out a little and show signs of wrinkling, or worse – a complete indent, the specimen is older."

Carrie carefully turned the bat over, revealing a strip of yellow foam. "I created a foam cast of Benny after carefully noting his measurements. After measuring him, I washed, treated and tanned him and am now putting the finishing touches on his new forever body."

"Fascinating," Jo murmured. "He looks as if he's going to fly away."

"Or suck blood from our necks," Delta joked.

"Bats are completely misunderstood," Carrie said. "They're an important part of our ecosystem. They control the mosquito population and are critical pollinators of seeds and fruits."

"I'll take your word for it," Delta said. "So, Benny is almost ready to go home?

"Yep. After I finish adding Benny's voice and sculpting his back, I'll add some touch-ups using paint or airbrushing."

Jo consulted her watch. "That was an interesting lesson. Thank you, Carrie. We should be going."

Delta and Jo began making their way to the door. Carrie hurried after them. "Are you sure you can't stay for a cup of coffee or tea?"

"Maybe next time." Jo smiled. "I'm looking forward to seeing your special creation for the kids' Christmas party."

"It will be worth the wait," Carrie promised before thanking them for stopping by.

Delta spoke after they pulled out of her driveway. "I think the woman's been sniffing a little too much formaldehyde." She twirled a finger next to her forehead.

"She strikes me as lonely," Jo said. "What do you think about Pastor Murphy?"

"I suppose anything is possible. Harrison Cantwell had a knack for getting under the skin of even the most mild-mannered person."

"Including Carrie's skin. Nash told me about how Harrison and Carrie's husband, Abner, liked to hang out at a local bar. Carrie finally got fed up and confronted them. Harrison followed her home, and Abner had to call the cops."

"I plum forgot all about that." Delta whistled loudly. "Talk about Fourth of July fireworks. Carrie ended up getting a restraining order on Harrison. It was a mess."

"Harrison was giving her a hard time the other day at the DABO meeting, making fun of her," Jo said. "Maybe she confronted him after the meeting ended, they fought and she killed him."

"It's possible."

"I hate to say it, but Pastor Murphy has moved up on the list of suspects, and so has Carrie."

"I don't think the Maltons, Marlee or Claire are suspects," Delta said.

"Which leaves the number one suspect as me and perhaps even Pastor Murphy."

"And Carrie."

"Unfortunately, I think I'm near the top of the list." Jo pondered the new information. "We still have to figure out who's hanging around the farm. I was thinking...I know the perfect person who might be able to help."

Chapter 19

"Are you sure you want my help?" Raylene cleared her throat. "It's been years since I've tracked someone down."

"Except for the time you helped me figure out who murdered the employee at Marlee's deli and cleared Sherry's name," Jo reminded her.

"But you had that half-solved before I came on board."

"Still, you were instrumental in helping me track down the real killer," Jo insisted. "I told you there's footage of someone or something moving past the surveillance camera last night. Whether the shadow was a person or an unexplained apparition, the fact is someone is lurking nearby."

"Not to mention someone tampered with the vending machine," Delta said. "My gut tells me it was the woman who escaped prison."

"It's a solid theory," Raylene agreed. "She was the one asking questions about the farm. You also said she was spotted at a local gas station."

"But why is she hanging around?" Jo asked. "The only thing I can think of is Tara told her what she was telling all of you. That I have money."

"Maybe she thinks you have a cash stash somewhere here at the farm," Delta said.

"That's crazy."

"Is it? If you escaped from prison, were on the run and desperate for money, wouldn't you go for the easiest means of getting your hands on it? Especially if your friend told you exactly where to find it."

"If Tara called me back, I would ask her myself exactly what she's done."

"You could try her again," Delta suggested.

"I guess it couldn't hurt." Jo ran to her office, grabbed her cell phone and returned to the kitchen. She dialed Tara's number. Much to Jo's surprise, the woman answered.

"Hello?"

"Tara?"

"Hi, Jo."

Jo detected a tremor in the woman's voice. "Is everything all right? Are you okay?"

"I...yeah. I'm all right." There was a long moment of silence. "I messed up, didn't I?"

"The truth of it is — you did. I'm sure your probation officer has issued a warrant for your arrest. If...or should I say *when* they find you, you'll be returning to Central."

"I know. I just..." Tara sighed heavily. "I fell apart. The decorations, the tree. I was desperate to go home." There were mournful sobs on the other end of the line, and despite all Tara had put Jo through, her heart went out to her.

"I know it was hard, but we could've talked. We could've worked through it."

"Can you put in a good word for me?" The woman sniffled.

"My hands were tied the moment you left the farm and broke the terms of your probation."

"I'm sorry, Jo. I never meant to cause you any trouble."

"But you have," Jo said softly. "What do you know about Karen Griffin?"

"I...I don't want to talk about her."

"Is she with you?"

"No. She's...I don't know where she is."

Jo switched tactics. "Someone has been messing around the farm. They tried to break into the vending machine, they broke the security lights and we caught someone on the surveillance camera."

"Really?"

Even though Tara asked the question, Jo got the impression she wasn't surprised. "Is Karen hanging around here, looking for money?"

The silence on the other end of the line told Jo everything she needed to know. "The women told me you were snooping around in my past. I think you planned to leave the farm some time ago. You somehow managed to help your friend escape, and now she's hanging around Divine, looking for something." Jo waited for a reply. "Tara?"

There was silence.

"Tara?" Jo stared at the phone. "She hung up on me."

"Because you were getting a little too close for comfort," Raylene said. "Are Tara and the escapee together?"

"She told me that they weren't. She knows she messed up. I think Karen is hanging around here looking for some quick cash, which is where you come in." Jo motioned to Raylene. "Well? Will you help me?"

Raylene studied the floor before lifting her head and meeting Jo's questioning gaze. "I'll help, but there are no guarantees."

"I'm not asking for one."

"Our first move is to find out a little more about Karen Griffin, her motivation, her habits, what makes her tick."

Delta spoke. "Money is her motivator. She took out an insurance policy, killed her husband in a home fire and tried to collect."

"That's pretty serious," Raylene said.

"Which means if she's desperate to get her hands on some quick cash and she thinks I have some here at the farm, we're an attractive target."

"What I can't figure out is how she's getting around." Delta leaned her hip on the counter. "She would need some sort of transportation."

"It isn't Tara. She doesn't have a car. There has to be another person involved," Jo said.

"Her next move might be trying to break into the house." Raylene drummed her fingers on the table. "Like I said, I need to gather information and put a profile together so we can try to anticipate her next move."

"Wait a minute!" Jo snapped her fingers. "I have an idea who might be able to help us out."

"Pastor Murphy," Delta guessed.

"Bingo. He's met a lot of the incarcerated women. He may have met Karen." Jo consulted the clock. "He mentioned he planned to spend part of today at the church sorting through the rest of the toys before bringing them by this evening."

"We could wait until he gets here tonight," Delta said.

"We'll lose precious time if we wait until nightfall," Jo shook her head. "If Karen is targeting us, she has the advantage of the cover of darkness, which puts us on the defensive."

"I'll ride over there with you," Raylene said.

Delta got busy making dinner while Jo and Raylene headed out.

When they reached the church parking lot, Jo eased the truck into an empty spot next to Pastor Murphy's van. "Let's try the sanctuary first."

The lobby entrance was locked. Jo cupped her hands to her eyes and peered through the glass. "There's a light on in the back. Let's circle around."

The women retraced their steps, making their way down the sidewalk to the back of the building.

"This is Pastor Murphy's office." Jo rapped lightly on the door. No one answered. "Maybe he isn't here."

"I think I heard something." Raylene motioned for Jo to follow her to the side of the building, where they found the pastor frowning at a row of kids' bikes.

"Hello, Pastor Murphy," Jo called out as they drew closer.

The pastor turned, a smile lighting his face. "Hello, Jo. Raylene."

"Look at all of those bikes," Jo said.

"It's the number one request on the kids' wish lists. I'm trying to figure out how I'm going to load all of these in my van."

"As luck would have it, I drove the truck today," Jo said. "I can bring a bunch back with me."

"Jo to the rescue once again. That would be wonderful."

They each grabbed a bike and began walking it to the truck. Jo lowered the tailgate. "I'll load them if you bring them to me."

The pastor and Raylene moved back and forth, bringing bikes while Jo lined them up in the truck's bed.

"How many more?" Jo eyed the bed as she stepped onto the tailgate. "We're running out of room."

"This is the last one." Raylene lifted a small bike.

The pastor waited for Jo to hop down. "I'm sure you didn't come here to take a load of bikes home."

"No. I'm here because someone is targeting the farm. We believe it may be the woman who escaped from the women's prison, Karen Griffin."

"Let's chat in my office." Pastor Murphy and the women returned to the back and to his office. "Have a seat. Sheriff Franklin was here yesterday asking about Karen Griffin."

"You know her?" Jo asked.

"I met with her several times. She's a troubled woman."

"Troubled?"

"I…" The pastor abruptly stopped.

"What is it?"

"I'm sorry, Jo. This is an issue of clergy-penitent. In other words, it's a matter of clergy confidentiality."

"Your conversations are private," Jo said.

"Exactly. As with any conversation with the incarcerated, I'm bound by my oath to respect their privacy."

"But you've come to me several times discussing inmates' private issues when recommending them for the farm."

"With our permission," Raylene answered.

"Raylene is correct. With each of your residents, I obtained their permission to discuss their situation with you."

"I see. That makes sense. The reason I'm asking about Ms. Griffin is because I think she's targeting me...targeting us and the farm." Jo told him about the string of recent incidents, starting with the damage to the vending machine, the piece of torn fabric Gary found on the side of the shed and the image the surveillance camera captured the previous night. "Sherry is certain Griffin was in the deli a couple of days ago asking questions about the farm. I already know how she ended up in prison but was looking for more details."

"In other words, what makes her tick," Raylene chimed in.

The pastor leaned back in the chair and clasped his hands. "I can't share privileged information, but I can try to steer you in the right direction. Ms. Griffin's case was highly publicized in the Wichita area a few years back. An online search might reveal more of her background, the story of what happened and how she ended up in prison."

"That's an excellent idea," Jo said. "We'll do that."

"I wish I could help you more. I will say, and you'll find this out after you do some digging around, is that you have cause for concern if Ms. Griffin is targeting you."

Jo's breath caught in her throat. "Meaning we may be in danger."

"It's possible." The pastor lifted his hands. "I've already said too much. The local authorities are searching for her and Tara. Until she...they are apprehended, my recommendation to you is to be on your guard."

"We are." Jo slowly stood. She thought about the conversation with Carrie Ford, how Pastor Murphy had worked alongside Eileen Cantwell, the woman who had somehow misread their relationship and had fallen in love with him.

He walked a fine line between compassion, caring and confidentiality. It was a line Jo wasn't sure she could handle. "I asked for Raylene's help since she has experience in tracking this kind of person down."

"It sounds as if you won't have far to go." The pastor accompanied them out of his office and to the parking lot. "Thank you for taking these bikes for me. I'll be by with the next load of toys after supper."

"We'll be waiting. Would you like us to help you load them in your van before we leave?"

"I appreciate your generous offer. I have more tagging and sorting to do. This is a big project, even for a small army."

"We'll help in any way we can," Jo said.

"You've already done so much," the pastor said. "I still can't believe you found the toys."

"I can't either."

"Jo is turning into a super sleuth," Raylene teased.

"Which means if anyone can find out who's targeting your farm, it will be you two." The pastor waited for the women to climb into the truck and back out of the church's driveway before returning inside.

When they reached the farm, Jo and Raylene, along with Nash, unloaded the bikes and then made their way to Jo's office.

"Where did Pastor Murphy say the crime occurred?" Jo turned her computer on and double-clicked on the search screen.

"Wichita."

Jo typed in Karen Griffin, Wichita, Kansas. Several search results appeared. She clicked on the one at the top. The story was recent, only a couple of days old. "Arsonist and husband killer, Karen Griffin, escapes Central State Penitentiary."

Jo read the story aloud.

"Local authorities are scouring the area, searching for Central State Penitentiary escapee, Karen Griffin. A Department of Corrections official who agreed to speak on the condition of anonymity claimed a brief lapse in guard duties during shift rotation created an opportunity for the inmate, who was on light kitchen duty, to escape."

She scrolled the screen. "According to our source, the daring escape happened in the early evening. Prison officials also believe the inmate had some outside assistance." She paused.

"What is it?" Raylene asked.

"Smith County residents are asked to remain on alert for possible sightings of the woman." Jo shifted the computer. "Here's a picture of her."

Raylene scooted forward. "She looks angry."

"Yes, she does. Angry and on the run." Jo began to read the last sentence, the one that gave her chill bumps.

Chapter 20

"They believe whoever assisted in Ms. Griffin's escape is armed, and they're both considered extremely dangerous." Jo exited the screen and clicked on the next article. The second story was similar to the first but also included a backstory of the original crime.

"What does it say?" Raylene asked.

Jo skimmed the highlights. "Griffin took out a large life insurance policy on her husband. Days before the fire, there were several incidents of vandalism near the couple's home, which are now believed to have been perpetrated by Griffin to throw authorities off. During the night in question, Karen claimed she had gone out for the evening with friends. Her husband was home and asleep when she returned."

"She went to bed but forgot to set the home alarm. Sometime during the night, she woke to the fire. She tried to rouse her husband, but the fire spread quickly, forcing her to flee through a bedroom window."

Jo pressed a light hand to her chest. "By the time firefighters arrived at the scene, the home was completely engulfed. During the trial, Griffin denied any involvement."

"So maybe she was innocent."

"Hang on. There's one more paragraph. Karen Griffin changed her story after her murder conviction. Attorneys have filed new papers, arguing she was a victim of domestic abuse."

"She was convicted, and then she changed her story," Raylene said.

"In a nutshell," Jo said. "In her new story, Griffin says she and her husband argued the night of the fire. She left the house. He went to bed. When she returned, she claims a voice told her to set the house on fire."

"Seriously?" Raylene asked. "She's going for an insanity plea or self-defense."

"Or maybe a combination of the two." Jo skimmed the rest of the story and leaned back in the chair. "It sounds as if she's mentally unstable."

"Extremely. If she's targeting the farm, who's to say she won't hear voices telling her to kill all of us?"

"This is even more disturbing than I imagined," Jo could feel a sudden panic well up inside her. They were sitting ducks. "We need to figure out if she's targeting the farm."

"What about the sheriff's department?" Raylene asked.

"They stepped up patrols. We have no proof she's the one hanging around. Not to mention they have their hands full trying to figure out who murdered Harrison Cantwell."

"We're on our own."

"Basically."

"We're both in agreement the woman is mentally unstable, which is what Pastor Murphy alluded to. Let's go with she was a victim of domestic abuse. Something inside her snapped. She justified her husband's death, and maybe she was crazy enough that a small voice was telling her to kill her husband."

"But not crazy enough not to plan ahead and take out a hefty life insurance policy on him," Jo pointed out.

"Right. So she's crazy, yet conniving," Raylene said. "She feels she's been wrongly imprisoned. Somehow, she escapes. She comes to Divine..."

"Because of Tara," Jo interrupted.

"Because of Tara. It's possible they're together, although Tara's goal was to make it to Chicago." Raylene rubbed a hand across her brow. "I think the authorities are right and there's another person involved."

"Someone with a means of transportation," Jo said.

"If they had a vehicle, why hang around here? Why not go rob a bank?"

"I don't know."

"We need to search the property," Raylene said.

"We've already done that."

"You may have missed something...some small clue."

"It certainly won't hurt to have a fresh set of experienced eyes look around."

Jo and Raylene stopped by the kitchen, where they found Delta standing in front of the stove. "You find anything out about that woman?"

"We did. She has mental issues," Jo grabbed her jacket off the hook. "And she's dangerous. Raylene and I are going to search for clues."

The women traipsed across the driveway to the shed. Jo used her master key to open the door and stood off to the side, watching Raylene search the interior.

She worked her way from left to right, top to bottom, removing items and inspecting contents. Raylene grabbed a flashlight off the shelf and shined it under the cabinets.

After she finished, she joined Jo in the doorway. "This place is clean. Where did Gary find the piece of cloth?"

"Over here." Jo led her behind the shed.

Raylene studied the corner of the building and then shifted her gaze to the road. "It would be fairly easy for someone to sneak onto the property without being seen. You said the surveillance cameras caught a shadowy figure. Which camera?"

"It was the one in front of the bakeshop and mercantile." Jo led her to the building and pointed up. "This one."

Raylene tilted her head, studying the camera. She stepped forward until she was standing directly beneath it. "The person or object came from the direction of the mercantile, toward the bakeshop and disappeared somewhere in the parking lot."

"Heading in the direction of the house," Jo added.

"Can you re-enact the movement of the shadowy figure?"

"I can." Jo joined Raylene on the porch. She spread her arms out and drifted across the gravel parking lot.

Raylene chuckled. "What are you doing?"

"Mimicking the shadowy figure."

"They had their hands in the air?"

"I think so." Jo's arms fell to her side. "You should check it out."

"I think I should," Raylene teased. "Although your re-enactment was entertaining."

The women found Nash in the workshop, paintbrush in hand, brushing large strokes across the side of Santa's sleigh.

"Lookin' good," Jo said.

"Right back atcha," Nash flirted.

Jo's cheeks warmed, and she shook her head. "I meant the sleigh."

"I know what you meant," he grinned. "What are you doing?"

"Showing Raylene the surveillance footage from last night." The computer in Nash's office was already on. Jo clicked the surveillance camera app and pulled up the previous night's recordings. It took her a few minutes to find the exact location. "This is it."

Raylene studied the shadowy figure. "It captured the image at two-twenty this morning. Did you check surveillance cameras from previous nights?"

"Nash did. This was the only thing he found. There was nothing on the house cameras."

"Hmm." Raylene pressed the play button again and paused it when the shadowy figure was midway across the screen. "What about the figure in the corner of the screen?"

"What figure?"

"This one." Raylene tapped the screen.

"I don't see anything."

"I'll enlarge it." Raylene zoomed in on the image.

Jo could barely make out a set of glowing eyes and the outline of a person's head. They were staring straight at the shadowy figure.

"Now, do you see it?"

"I do," Jo whispered. "There was more than one person out here last night."

"That appears to be the case."

"Nash!" Jo darted to the door and motioned for him to join them. "We missed something on the surveillance video from last night."

"We did?" Nash strode into his office.

"It's in the corner."

He leaned in. "You're right. It looks like someone is lurking near the corner of the building. Good eye, Raylene."

"Thanks."

"Let's finish searching the area," Jo said as they stepped out of Nash's office.

"Have you noticed anything near the house?" Raylene asked.

"No." Jo shook her head. "Duke and I slept downstairs last night. He would've alerted me to anything even remotely close by."

Raylene shoved her hands in her pockets. "The woman has been spotted in town at the deli and the gas station."

"Correct," Jo said.

"What about here?"

"At the farm?"

"The mercantile and bakeshop," Raylene said. "Have you shown the women a picture of Karen Griffin?"

"I...no. Do you think she would be bold enough to come here in broad daylight?"

"Bold...or, as we both agreed, crazy," Raylene said.

"True. I'll be right back." Jo dashed to her office. She pulled up the news article, which included a picture of Karen Griffin and then printed a screenshot.

Jo caught up with Raylene near the front steps. Their first stop was the mercantile, where Kelli and Michelle were working. Jo showed them the picture of the woman, but neither of them recognized her.

The next stop was the bakeshop, where Leah had taken over so that Raylene could help Jo. They waited for a customer to finish paying for her purchases and approached the counter.

Jo handed the printout to Leah. "Have you seen this woman in the store recently?"

"No. I don't think so." Leah started to hand it back and then stopped. "Wait a minute." She used two fingers to cover the bottom of the woman's hair. "Yeah. I think I did. It was yesterday. Her hair was shorter, though."

"What did she do?"

"She asked if we were hiring. I told her we weren't, but that the deli in town might be."

"Then what happened?" Jo asked.

"She left the store and went outside. She stood there for a few minutes kind of looking around."

"Casing the joint," Raylene said.

"There's something else I remember," Leah said. "She had a bruise on her cheek."

Chapter 21

"Sherry said the same thing," Jo whispered. "She mentioned Karen Griffin had a bruise on her cheek."

"Did you see where she went?" Raylene asked. "Did she get in a car and drive off?"

"I don't know. I was going to ask her if she needed something else, but a customer asked for help. By the time I looked again, she was gone."

Jo thanked Leah for the information, and she and Raylene stepped onto the front porch. "I think this is confirmation Karen Griffin is in the vicinity. Let's head out back to the gardens."

The women fell into step and trekked to the smaller garden first.

Raylene approached the edge. "A fresh snowfall would help."

"It's cold enough to snow." Jo shivered as a stiff wind whipped across the open field, and she tugged on the zipper of her jacket.

They finished inspecting the garden before making their way to the second, larger one. Adjacent to the garden was a rusted grain silo.

"I can't imagine anyone hiding out in here." Jo dropped to her knees and grabbed the door handle. It scraped loudly against the cement floor as she forced it up. "This thing hasn't been opened in months."

Raylene waited until Jo closed the door and motioned to the wooden fence. "What's back there?"

"Our neighbor, Dave Kilwin's farm, is to the left. Kansas Creek Reservation borders us on the other side."

"The Native American reservation," Raylene said.

"Yes. Those are the only two properties abutting ours."

"How far away is it...the reservation I mean?"

"Not far. Our farm is only ten acres. The reservation is much larger."

"Which might make a perfect hiding spot for someone who is on the run," Raylene said.

"I hadn't thought about that." Jo began chewing on her lower lip. "The reservation isn't governed by our laws."

"But the authorities would have questioned them about Karen Griffin," Raylene pointed out.

"I'm sure they have. Like I said, they own a lot of land. Let's take a drive over there. I know Chief Tallgrass and Storm Runner. He's one of the reservation's patrolling officers."

The women returned to the front of the property. Jo ran inside to grab her purse while Raylene waited in the truck.

It was a quick drive from the farm to the reservation. Jo missed the main entrance and had to backtrack. "I almost forgot how to get here." She drove through the open gates and circled the main shopping area before pulling into a parking spot in front of the gift shop.

"Let's try the gift shop first." Jo approached the woman behind the counter. "We're looking for Chief Tallgrass or Storm Runner."

"The chief is out for the day. Storm Runner is working. He has a radio. Would you like me to call him?"

"Please. Could you tell him that his neighbor, Joanna Pepperdine, would like to speak with him?"

Jo and Raylene waited for the woman to make the call.

She set the radio on the counter. "Storm Runner is on his way. He will meet you out front."

"Thank you." The women stepped out of the shop. They didn't have long to wait before a patrol car pulled in next to Jo's truck.

Storm Runner climbed out with a wide smile on his face. "Joanna."

"Hello, Storm Runner." Jo shook his hand and motioned to Raylene. "This is one of my residents, Raylene."

"It's nice to meet you."

"Same here."

"I was telling my wife, Namid, we need to stop back by the bakeshop for more of Delta's Divine Raspberry Bars." He patted his stomach. "What can I do for you?"

"We believe a recent prison escapee may be targeting my farm and were wondering if you've seen her." Jo pulled the folded sheet of paper with the woman's mugshot from her pocket and handed it to him.

He glanced at the picture before handing it back. "Sheriff Franklin from Smith County stopped by here a couple of days ago asking about her. We have not seen anyone matching this description, but now that you mention it, I did notice someone had started a fire in one of the outbuildings last night."

Jo's heart skipped a beat. "Was it anywhere near our property border?"

"It was. I will show you. We can take my car." The women climbed into the back of the patrol car, and Storm Runner drove them away from the main area. They made several turns before turning onto a narrow, rutted dirt path.

"Are you sure we're not driving around in circles?" Jo joked.

"We are almost there," Storm Runner glanced in the rearview mirror. "It is near the corner of the property, far away from our main compound."

The car crested a small hill, and a dilapidated cabin appeared on the horizon. "We will have to park here and walk the rest of the way."

The officer exited the vehicle and then opened the back door for the women to get out. "I've always wanted to ride in the back of a patrol car," Jo said.

"You weren't missing anything," Raylene said. "I would be perfectly happy if I never saw the back of a police car again in my life."

The officer's long strides left Jo and Raylene several yards behind.

They picked up the pace and caught up with him as he reached the front of the small cabin. On closer inspection, Jo could see cracks in the lap siding. An abandoned wasp's nest was nestled in the corner of the overhang.

The front door hung haphazardly, creating a large, gaping opening at the bottom.

"I will check it first."

Raylene and Jo waited for Storm Runner to signal the coast was clear. They followed him inside, where the smell of smoke lingered in the air. "As I mentioned, someone started a fire in the fireplace."

The trio crossed the barren room and approached a small brick fireplace, where a black kettle hung from a metal hook.

Storm Runner placed his hand on the side of the pot. "It is still warm."

"Which means the fire was recent."

"I think it was last night." Storm Runner stood. "Sometimes, we get teenagers messing around, so I check the buildings every couple of days."

"They come all the way out here?" The floor creaked loudly as Jo wandered to the window overlooking the porch.

"They come back here thinking no one will catch them," he said. "I also found a set of tracks."

Jo and Raylene stepped out of the building and watched as Storm Runner struggled to close the door. "It is an old building. We are planning to tear it down next spring. The tracks are over here."

They traipsed down the small hill and several yards away from the structure before Storm Runner abruptly stopped. He pointed at the ground. "These are fresh tracks."

Jo dropped to one knee and inspected the imprint. "It looks like a small tennis shoe."

"The trail is heading that way." Storm Runner pointed straight ahead. "Your farm is over the next hill. With a pair of binoculars, we would be able to see your beehives in the corner of the property. I did not follow the tracks, but we can now." He didn't wait for an answer and began walking in the direction of Jo's farm.

The trio climbed a small hill and continued walking until they reached a chain link fence and a metal gate. "On the other side of this gate is a trail that leads to your property. Ten more minutes and we would be there."

"This woman, the escapee, has been spotted on our property. I believe she may be the one hiding out here."

"What can we do to help?" Storm Runner asked.

"I think she's going to make a move soon, either today or tomorrow. She's becoming bolder, and I'm afraid she's growing desperate and more dangerous."

"Desperate and dangerous are a lethal combination. You would like us to keep an eye out to see if it is her and if she returns."

"If you don't mind. We'll be doing the same. Perhaps between the two of us, we can catch her before someone gets hurt."

Storm Runner nodded somberly. "We will help our friend and neighbor. I will have my men stake out this area today and tonight."

"And we'll be doing the same," Jo pressed her palms together. "She may also have an accomplice, and they may be armed."

"My men will be well advised."

They returned to the patrol car and the front of the reservation. Storm Runner followed Jo to the truck. "I will take your cell phone number and give you mine so we can remain in contact."

"That's a great idea." Jo added him to her list of cell phone contacts and then rattled off her number. "Thank you, again, Storm Runner."

"You are welcome. I am sure with all of us on patrol, we will find out who is trespassing."

Raylene glanced in the side mirror as they drove off. "Do you think we can catch her...if it's even her?"

"I hope so. I'm almost a hundred percent certain it's her. Who else could it be? A fire in an abandoned shack. Small footprints leading toward our property. Leah confirmed she was in the store.

There was also Sherry's sighting and the woman's curiosity about us."

Back at the farm, Jo called an emergency meeting. Everyone except for Leah and Michelle, who were working, gathered in front of the bakeshop.

Jo briefly told them all that had happened, how she suspected an unstable and potentially dangerous Karen Griffin was targeting the farm. She also filled them in on the visit to the Indian reservation and the conversation with Storm Runner.

"You believe she's going to try something again?" Kelli asked.

"I think she's desperate. She knows the authorities are searching for her, which is why she's been hiding out on the Indian reservation. She may be armed, and she may have an accomplice."

"Well, we got guns," Delta said.

"I also think it would be best for everyone to sleep in the main house tonight."

"Safety in numbers. Might not be a bad idea," Nash said.

With the decision made for all of the farm's residents to spend the night inside the house, the meeting ended.

Delta followed Jo into the kitchen. "You think the woman is off her rocker and hanging around here?"

"I...don't know what to think. I do know Leah talked to her, which means she's been on the property. Storm Runner showed us the small sneaker tracks he found not far from our property line."

"Not to mention Sherry said the woman was asking a lot of questions about us," Delta said. "I gotta believe this all leads back to Tara. No one has seen hide nor hair of her."

"They could've parted ways. That's what I think. I think Tara helped Karen escape. Something happened. Tara left the area, but Karen is still hanging around. I should touch base with Sheriff Franklin to let him know what we found." Jo switched her cell phone on and dialed the sheriff's number. To Jo's surprise, he answered the call.

"Sheriff Franklin speaking."

"Hello, Sheriff. This is Joanna Pepperdine. I'm calling to let you know one of our residents recognized Karen Griffin. She was in our bakeshop the other day."

Jo continued. "We also caught someone on our surveillance cameras last night. We believe she may be lurking around the farm or possibly hiding out at Kansas Creek Reservation. There's no indication Tara is with her."

"Ms. Cloyne is not with Karen Griffin," the sheriff said. "I was getting ready to call you."

Chapter 22

"Officers from the Chicago Police Department just arrested Tara Cloyne. She's being held there until we can arrange to have her transferred back to Kansas."

Jo blinked rapidly. "She made it to Chicago."

"They tracked her using the Tracfone number you gave us."

"I wonder if it was worth it," Jo said it as much to herself as to the sheriff. "She was desperate to see her daughter and her family."

"She was with them," the sheriff said. "When she showed up, the mother snuck off to call us. We were already closing in on her and in the neighborhood when the takedown took place."

"I believe Karen Griffin is still here in the Divine area. Tara may have valuable information."

"We plan to question her as soon as she's brought back to Kansas, but it might take a day or two. In the meantime, we'll continue with additional patrols."

"I appreciate that."

The sheriff ended the call, and Jo waved the phone in the air. "One down...two to go. Tara was picked up at her parent's place in Chicago."

*****

Jo was restless and on edge for the rest of the day. She picked at the food on her plate and barely joined in on the dinner conversation.

The pastor arrived shortly after the meal ended, and Jo offered to clean up while the others helped him unload the last of the Christmas gifts.

Delta wandered in as Jo was loading the dishwasher. "You look like you got the weight of the world on those thin shoulders."

"My mind is racing ninety miles an hour. I can't help but wonder if Karen Griffin and Harrison Cantwell's death are somehow linked."

"How would the two of them have crossed paths?" Delta asked.

"I don't know. I can't shake the feeling there's a connection." Jo turned the dishwasher on. "Maybe I'll figure it out. In the meantime, we better see if they need help in the barn."

Pastor Murphy caught Jo's eye as soon as she stepped inside. "Delta told me the police found Tara in Chicago, but Karen Griffin is still on the run."

"She's here."

"Here?" The pastor's eyes grew wide. "You saw her?"

"Leah said she was in the bakeshop asking about employment the other day. She tried to disguise her appearance by chopping off her hair, but we're almost certain it was her." Jo told him about her visit to the Indian reservation and her conversation with Storm Runner. "I think she's hiding out at the reservation, knowing the local police have no jurisdiction and can't search for her there."

"And she's coming back here at night to do what?"

"To case the place so she can rob us?" Jo shrugged. "The sheriff has stepped up area patrols, but they would still have to be in the right spot at the right time."

"I'm sorry to hear that, Jo. I wish there was something I could do."

"We'll get through it," Jo forced a smile. "In the meantime, I have plenty to keep me busy."

"With all of this." He motioned to the mountain of wrapped presents and the decorations Nash and Gary had worked so hard on.

"Yes, and we've loved every minute of it."

After Pastor Murphy left, the women returned to their units to gather their personal belongings and Curtis.

Nash offered to sleep on the couch while the women doubled up in the bedrooms upstairs. Duke, excited to see everyone, raced up the stairs and from room to room.

Much to his dismay, Curtis was relegated to the kitchen area once again, far away from the Christmas tree and the twinkling lights.

Jo waited for the women to settle into their rooms before checking on Nash one final time. She perched on the edge of his makeshift bed. "Thanks for volunteering to sleep here tonight."

"You're welcome." Nash propped his pillow against the armrest. "You seem a little out of sorts tonight."

"Our lives have been turned upside down. I mean, just look at us." Jo shared her thoughts, how Karen Griffin's escape and Harrison Cantwell's death were somehow linked. "Maybe it's wishful thinking on my part. Anything to take the heat off me."

"You could be onto something. You have a nose for this kind of thing."

"It seems like I'm getting a lot of practice." Jo changed the subject. "The Santa sleigh and reindeer project are almost complete."

"They are," Nash beamed. "We're almost done. I even managed to track down some sleigh bells. I figure by tomorrow afternoon, Gary and I will be ready for the big reveal."

"We could make a party out of it," Jo said. "The costumes are sitting in my office. I haven't had a chance to unpack the boxes. At least one project is moving forward, thanks to you."

"It was your Divine inspiration," Nash softly teased. "Bad things don't always happen to good people, but you've certainly had more than your fair share, especially lately."

"I have." Jo's shoulders slumped. "Maybe I'm crisis-fatigued."

Nash placed a light hand under Jo's chin. "Keep your chin up, soldier. It will all turn out for the best."

Their eyes met, and Nash leaned in for a long, lingering kiss. The kiss ended, leaving Jo breathless. She said the first thing that popped into her head. "You forgot the mistletoe again."

"You're right. I need to put it at the top of my shopping list." Nash pulled Jo to her feet and walked her to the bottom of the stairs.

"Holler if you need help." Jo took a tentative step before turning back. "Please be careful."

"I will," Nash promised as he patted Duke's head. "Duke and I will be on alert."

It took Jo a long time to fall asleep. She thought about Harrison Cantwell's death, how he stole the gifts from the church and planned to sue Jo for a bogus food poisoning claim.

She also thought about how he sent a check to the pastor for the children's toys. Had he had a change of heart right before his death? Why not return the toys...unless he was too ashamed to admit what he'd done?

She thought about Harrison's wife, Eileen, and how she'd fallen in love with the pastor and then committed suicide. Harrison harbored hatred toward the pastor, blaming him for his wife's death. Had Pastor Murphy confronted Harrison, they argued and the pastor accidentally killed him?

Jo couldn't rule out Carrie Ford, who had a motive, as well. There was some bad blood between her and Harrison, enough that the cops had been called, and Carrie had secured a restraining order.

She remembered the incident in the restaurant, how Harrison had belittled Carrie. Perhaps she'd become fed up with him and shot him.

She also thought about Karen Griffin. The woman was obviously disturbed and targeting Jo, but why? Was it because of money? Had Tara told her Jo was loaded, motivating the woman to hang around until she could get her hands on cash?

But Jo didn't keep cash at the house. True, she kept a small amount in a safe in her room for emergencies, but it was only a few hundred dollars and certainly not enough to risk robbing someone.

Then there was Tara who would soon be returning to Central to finish out her sentence. Perhaps the judge would even extend it.

Tara had apologized to Jo, which was the right thing to do, but she had hurt herself more than anyone. There was more to the story, and Jo vowed to get to the bottom of it as soon as she was back at Central.

The air needed to be cleared, and Jo intended to do that, one way or the other. At the very least, she needed to impress upon Tara that it was dangerous to go around telling others, particularly incarcerated inmates, she was keeping loads of cash.

It was a fitful night as Jo woke at every creak and pop, certain someone was trying to break into the house – or even more horrifying – attempting to burn it to the ground with everyone inside.

Thump. Jo sat straight up, straining to listen. She heard the sound again, echoing through the register ducts. She reached for her robe and tiptoed down the stairs.

The couch was empty. Duke sat in front of the door staring at it intently.

"Nash?" Jo whispered.

"Over here." Nash emerged from the shadows.

"What's going on? I thought I heard a noise."

"Duke heard it, too." Nash lifted the corner of the curtain. "I saw someone go around the back of the barn about ten minutes ago. I called the cops. They're on the way."

"Is there only one person?" Jo peered anxiously out the window.

"I don't know. Maybe they got spooked and took off." Nash grabbed Jo's arm. "Hang on. I see lights."

Jo craned her neck and caught a glimpse of bright lights as they flashed across the side of Nash's workshop. "Someone is out there."

The faint sound of sirens grew louder. "The police are here." Through the lace curtains, Jo watched as a sheriff's patrol car careened into the driveway. Another patrol car flew in behind the first one, the car's headlights illuminating the front of Jo's barn and her neighbor, Storm Runner.

Chapter 23

Things moved fast as the officers scrambled out of the cars and ran toward the barn.

"It looks like they have someone cornered." Nash waited until the scene was secure and sprinted down the porch steps, taking long strides until he reached the men standing in front of one of the patrol cars.

There was a commotion nearby, and Jo realized there was someone face down on the ground.

"What's going on?"

Jo jumped at the sound of Delta's voice in her ear. "You scared me half to death."

"Sorry. I thought you heard me. What's going on?" Delta repeated as she joined Jo on the porch.

"Nash called the cops after Duke alerted him to someone outside. I think they caught whoever it was."

"I see Sheriff Franklin leaning against the side of his car." Delta slipped past Jo.

"Wait for me." Jo followed Delta to the trio of officers who were standing in a semi-circle. She took a tentative step closer, not surprised to discover the handcuffed person flopping around on the ground was Karen Griffin. "You can't leave me down here. I'll sue you for bodily injury."

"Hold your horses, Ms. Griffin. You'll be leaving soon enough," the sheriff calmly replied.

The woman let out a string of expletives, cursing the sheriff, Storm Runner and even Jo. "You better keep them away from me."

"These people aren't going to hurt you." Two deputies stepped in on each side of the woman and pulled her to her feet.

"Not them. The giant men on the porch who were chasing me."

Jo shook her head, confused. "What men?"

"The ones who chased me out of the yard. I don't know where they went."

"Must be some good drugs you're on." One of the deputies shook his head.

"I'm not on anything," Griffin insisted. "You must've seen them." The woman continued to argue as they escorted her to the back of the patrol car.

Jo watched them place her inside. "Just as I suspected, it was her lurking around here all of this time."

"One of our guys was close by when Nash called. Thanks to Storm Runner and his men, she didn't get far." The sheriff motioned to Storm Runner. "How did you end up on her trail?"

"Ms. Pepperdine stopped by yesterday to tell us about some suspicious activity around her place.

We had also noticed someone on our property, at an old cabin not far from here. One of my men was watching the cabin tonight. He spotted her a couple of hours ago. I assembled a team and started tracking her. She was on the move and heading toward Joanna's farm."

Storm Runner told them they lost sight of her near the fence line. "By the time we reached the back of the barn, she was on the run, but running toward us. She was yelling something about not letting them get her."

"She thought someone was chasing her," Jo said.

"She said they were giants. We did not see them – only her."

One of Storm Runner's men cleared his throat. "I did see a large man. He was about fifty yards from her and moving fast. She passed by under the mercury light. He didn't. It's almost as if he vanished."

The sheriff held up a hunting knife. "She had this and a lockpick set in her pocket."

"She was getting ready to break in," Jo said.

"It looks as if she and her friend, Tara Cloyne, are about to be reunited in prison." The sheriff motioned to his men. "Go get Rusty. I want a perimeter search to make sure no one else is out there."

"Sure thing." The deputy opened the back door of his SUV patrol vehicle. "Time to get to work, Rusty."

A German shepherd K-9 bolted from the back. The deputy and K-9 hit the ground running.

"If someone is out there, Rusty will find 'em," the sheriff said confidently.

"Would you gentlemen like some coffee?" Delta asked.

"That's mighty hospitable of you, Delta." Sheriff Franklin shifted his feet. "I wouldn't mind a cup."

"Coffee it is. I'll be right back."

"We must return to the reservation," Storm Runner said. "Unless we are needed for questioning."

"You're free to leave," the sheriff said. "I'll swing by tomorrow to get a full statement for my report."

"Wait." Jo stopped Storm Runner. "Thank you for helping me."

"You are welcome. I am glad we were able to track the trespasser. She did not have good intentions."

"No, she did not." Jo thanked them again, and Storm Runner and his men faded into the darkness.

"I doubt Griffin had any idea they were even following her," Nash said.

"Not until it was too late." Jo lowered her voice. "What do you think about Griffin's claim?"

"The large men?" Nash asked. "Her mind may have been playing tricks on her. She's been on the run for several days."

319

"Or..."

"Or it could have been a Divine Intervention."

Delta returned with several to-go containers of coffee. The farm's residents trickled out of the house and stood, quietly talking on the porch.

Rusty and the deputy returned a short time later. "The place is clean," he said breathlessly. "Rusty picked up the woman's scent, but there was nothing else."

The sheriff turned to Jo. "Do you feel sufficiently safe if we leave?"

"Yes. You caught the culprit." She thanked the sheriff for his quick response and then waited for the men to depart while Delta and the residents returned inside.

Nash reached for Jo's hand, and they began making their way to the house. "I think we've had enough excitement for one day."

"And the rest of the year." Jo's scalp started to tingle, and she was filled with an overwhelming feeling they were being watched. She shot a quick glance over her shoulder.

"What is it?" Nash asked.

"I feel like we're being watched." Jo studied the barn and buildings but didn't see anything. "If Griffin was being chased by our guardian angels, they can stand guard as long as they want."

*****

It took another hour for everyone to settle down, and it was early dawn before they returned to bed.

Jo was wound up and knew there was no chance of her going back to sleep. After checking on Nash and Delta one final time, she crept up the stairs to her attic book nook.

She switched the table lamp on, casting a warm glow inside her cozy reading spot. Jo curled up in her favorite chair, tucking her feet beneath her before grabbing a book off the side table. She settled a soft throw around her legs and slipped her reading glasses on.

Jo quickly became absorbed in the story...a cozy mystery about an assistant cruise ship director who was hunting a killer on board the ship in the middle of the ocean. She read straight through and finished the book close to the time she typically woke.

She let out a low groan as she eased out of the chair, stiff from sitting in the same spot. Jo pressed a hand to her aching back and slid the book into an empty spot on the shelf before descending the narrow attic steps.

The smell of bacon frying wafted in the air, and she could hear laughter coming from downstairs. Jo made a beeline for her bathroom. As soon as she got ready, she joined the others in the kitchen.

Delta, who was standing in front of the stove, was the first to notice her. "You're the sleepyhead of the day."

"I never went back to bed. I've been reading in my book nook." Jo wandered to the kitchen counter and poured a cup of coffee. "I was too wound up to go back to sleep."

"Can't say as I blame you," Delta replied. "I'm hoping things are gonna start settling down around here."

After breakfast, the women gathered their belongings and carried them back to their units while Jo helped Delta clean the breakfast dishes.

"I'm going to run next door to check on Santa's workshop." Jo was almost there when a familiar vehicle pulled into the driveway. The driver climbed out and limped over.

"Hello, Miles."

"Hello, Jo. One of the employees at the motel said someone was looking for me. Based on her description, I thought it might have been you."

"It was." Jo pointed to an angry cut along his jawline. "Are you okay?"

Miles lightly touched his injury. "I'm fine. I got into a minor fender bender the other day."

Jo glanced at Miles's car, which didn't appear to be damaged. "In your car?"

"That? Uh. N-no. It was a loaner car," Miles stuttered. "My car was in the shop. Another driver ran a red light, and I was broadsided."

"I'm sorry to hear that. At least you're okay. The reason I was looking for you was to ask you about Harrison Cantwell. It appears he was getting ready to file a claim against me. I wondered if you knew anything about it since you were working with him."

"He was?" Miles's jaw dropped. "I had no idea."

"You didn't?"

"No." His eyes widened innocently. "I swear. I knew nothing about it. What sort of claim?"

"Food poisoning. He had even gone as far as to meet with an attorney. My guess is he planned to try to reach a cash settlement before filing the lawsuit but never got the chance."

"No. I swear to you, Jo. This is the first I've heard of him suing you."

"You may have to convince Sheriff Franklin of that. He's looking forward to talking to you."

"I have nothing to hide," Miles insisted. "I did not murder Cantwell as a favor to you or for any other reason. The motel can corroborate my whereabouts."

Jo softened her stance. "You must admit it doesn't look good. You had access to Cantwell, he ends up dead, you're related to me and Cantwell is in the process of suing me when you disappear."

"I didn't disappear. The motel employee you spoke to was wrong. I was still in the area." Miles changed the subject. "Now probably isn't the best time, but I wondered if you've had a chance to consider my request."

"I haven't," Jo admitted. "Between Cantwell's death and someone lurking about the farm causing chaos, not to mention the children's Christmas party, I've had my hands full."

"I heard about Santa's workshop, which is another reason I'm here." Miles reached inside his pocket, pulled out a check and handed it to Jo. "I would like to help. This is for the kids."

Jo glanced at the check. It was written out for fifty dollars.

"I wish I could give more, but money is kind of tight right now."

"I..." Jo attempted to hand it back. "The gifts have been covered. You don't need to do this."

"I don't need to. I want to."

"Then, thank you. I'll be sure to give it to Pastor Murphy." Jo folded the check in half. "Would you like to join us for the festivities?"

"Could I?" Miles brightened.

"It's this Saturday at six o'clock. We could always use an extra hand."

"I'll be here. Thanks for the invite. I'm on my way to the sheriff's station now to straighten this mess out."

Jo noted the pained expression on his face as he limped to his car. "You sure you're okay?"

"I'll be fine," Miles grimaced as he slid behind the wheel. "I figure a few more days and I'll be as good as new."

Jo stepped away from his car, watching as he gave her a wave good-bye and then pulled onto the road. "Miracles never do cease."

Chapter 24

"You sure you want to do this?" Pastor Murphy studied Jo's face.

"I do." She nodded firmly. "I think it's best for Tara and me to clear the air. If I wait too long, she may change her mind and refuse to see me."

It had been some time since Jo's last trip to Central. Her last visit was a face-to-face meeting with Tara when she was on the fence about allowing the woman to join the farm after her release.

Despite Jo's initial reluctance, she'd been impressed with Tara's desire to change her life so she could be reunited with her daughter.

Unfortunately, Tara's goal had also been her downfall. According to Pastor Murphy, she would not be granted another chance at early parole and would finish her sentence behind the walls of the women's prison, far from her daughter, her family and her freedom.

The pastor and Jo passed through the security checkpoint and made their way to the visiting area. Tara was already there. She hesitantly stood, as if unsure of what to do, her expression was a mixture of anxious and sad.

Jo's heart went out to the woman, and she wrapped her in a tight hug. "Tara. I'm glad to see you're all right." She released her grip and took a step back. "You're a little thinner for your adventure."

"It was a long trip. I'm so sorry, Jo," she whispered. "I never meant to cause you any trouble."

"Let's have a seat." Jo guided her to the nearby table. She sat next to Tara while Pastor Murphy took the seat across from her. "You were involved in Karen Griffin's escape. You left town to try to make it to Chicago. Karen stayed behind and began targeting the farm."

"It's my fault," Tara's lower lip started to tremble. "Her friend, Shawn, picked me up at the farm after everyone was asleep. We arranged to meet near the road."

"Using the cell phone you secretly purchased," Jo said.

"Yeah. It was so dumb. Dumb, dumb, dumb!" Tara's shoulders drooped.

"I'm not sure if you heard, but the authorities picked Shawn up yesterday after Karen told them where to find him. Let's go back to the night you left."

"Karen was already with Shawn when he picked me up. We spent the rest of the night sleeping in his car. The next day..." Tara's voice trailed off.

"What happened the next day?" the pastor prompted.

"I had no idea Shawn was gonna flip out."

"What do you mean by flip out?" Jo asked.

Tara clamped her mouth shut.

Jo decided to switch tactics. "How did you get money? The small amount you made from the farm wouldn't have lasted you very long."

Tara lowered her head and stared at her lap.

Jo leaned in. "Where did you get money, Tara?"

"A friend," Tara whispered.

"Shawn?"

Tara shook her head.

"Was it someone you met at the farm? Who was it?"

"I...I can't remember his name," Tara blurted out. "He was old. An old man. He showed up at the bakeshop, asking a lot of questions about you. He offered me money to take off my gloves and box up some baked goods. I thought it was weird until later."

Jo let out a gasp, feeling as if someone had punched her in the gut. "Harrison Cantwell?"

"I can't remember if he ever told me his name."

"So, you took the gloves off, boxed up his purchases and he left."

"Yes. Before he left, he told me there was a lot more where that came from and if I ever wanted to make some quick cash to come see him at the old theater in town," Tara said. "I told Karen and Shawn about him."

"Did you go there – to the theater, I mean?" Jo asked.

Silence.

"You did," Jo said. "You needed more money, so you went to the theater and met with Harrison Cantwell."

"I already told my probation officer. It was crazy. I had no idea Shawn would try to rob Cantwell, that he had a gun. I saw the gun, and Karen and I were like, no way. We took off." Tara shifted uncomfortably. "It was the same night we were splitting up. I hitched a ride to the bus station to make it to Chicago."

"You're aware Cantwell is dead. He was shot."

"I swear. I had no idea Shawn was going to kill him. Maybe he didn't. Maybe they fought for the gun, and it accidentally went off."

Jo leaned back in her chair. "Why was Karen targeting the farm?"

"I don't know," Tara replied in a small voice.

"I think you do know," Jo said. "I think someone told her I kept large sums of cash at the farm, making me an attractive target for a woman who was desperate to get money before fleeing the area."

The look on Tara's face told Jo everything she needed to know. She had hit the nail on the head for the reason the escapee was hanging around. "This could have been very bad for me and for the others at the farm. For the record, I do not have large sums of money at the farm."

Jo paused for a moment, choosing her next words very carefully. "I want to make one thing perfectly clear. I, along with Delta and Nash, will use whatever means necessary to protect our property from intruders and those who want to harm us."

Tara lowered her gaze.

"Am I making myself clear?"

"Perfectly," Tara solemnly nodded. "This doesn't look good for me, does it?"

"I'm no judge, but I think you may have gotten yourself into more trouble than you bargained for." Jo thanked her for telling her the truth and promised to pray for her.

Pastor Murphy and Jo were silent as they made their way out of the prison and returned to the pastor's vehicle.

"Don't be too hard on yourself, Jo. Tara obviously wasn't ready for early release."

"I'm guessing she'll be in there for a while now, possibly even longer than her original sentence."

"That's a safe assumption." The pastor checked the rearview mirror before backing out of the parking spot. "I have another inmate in mind. She's a really nice gal. A bit of a firecracker though. She'll liven your place up."

Jo rolled her eyes and groaned. "As if the farm needs any more livening up."

Chapter 25

"Quit picking at your beard." Delta swatted Santa's hand.

"It's itchy," Gary a/k/a Santa grunted. "It feels like someone glued sandpaper to the sides of my face and chin."

Jo grinned. "The kids should be here anytime now. You two need to stop fussing at each other and let me take some pictures before they get here." She motioned for Santa to climb into his custom-made sleigh.

Delta...Mrs. Claus eased in next to him and patted her red cap. "How does my cap look?"

"It's perfect," Jo said. "Smile." She snapped several photos of Santa and Mrs. Claus before directing the five merry elves to join them. The women gathered around the Clauses and the sleigh while Jo snapped away.

Nash stood off to the side, beaming with pride. Jo waved him in. "We need a few pictures of the Santa sleigh genius too."

They posed for more pictures, and then Miles, who had shown up to help, told Jo to join them.

He finished taking the pictures, and Jo reached for the camera. "Before the festivities begin, I wanted to have a private word with you."

"Sure." Miles followed her out of Santa's workshop.

Jo slowed when they reached the side entrance. "Thank you for pitching in to help out tonight."

"You're welcome. Thanks for including me. The place looks awesome. The kids are gonna love it."

"I couldn't have done it without Nash, Gary and Delta." Jo shoved her hands in her pockets. "I wanted to let you know I've changed my mind."

Miles lifted a brow.

"Welcome home. I mean, welcome to Divine."

"You're serious?" Miles gasped.

"I am." Jo nodded firmly. "If you want to stay in Divine, I'm not going to stop you."

Miles impulsively hugged her tightly, nearly giving Jo whiplash. "Sorry." He released his grip. "I didn't mean to do that. I just…"

"It's okay. I understand. In fact, I'm pretty sure I felt the same when I found out my offer on this place was accepted," she joked.

"You won't regret your decision. I promise."

"I'm sure I won't." Jo motioned toward the excited voices coming from Santa's workshop. "We better get back inside."

"Yes. Yes, of course."

Bright headlights flashed across the side of the building as a vehicle turned into the driveway. Jo squinted her eyes. "Oh, no."

"Is that the pastor?"

"No. He'll be arriving with a bus full of kids. It's someone else. Someone I completely forgot about," Jo groaned. "This ought to be interesting."

The red minivan coasted to a stop, and the driver's side door flew open. Carrie's high heels hit the gravel, and she began waving wildly. "Hey, Jo. I hope I'm not late." She tottered around the front of the minivan and to the sliding side door. "I could use a hand."

Jo and Miles joined Carrie, who had opened the door and was reaching inside.

"I almost didn't make it," she said breathlessly. "But I knew you were counting on me, and I couldn't let the children down." She carefully removed a wooden box and handed it to Miles. "One for you."

She reached back inside and pulled out an identical box. "And one for me."

Jo reluctantly slid the van door shut and followed Carrie and Miles into the workshop.

"Hellooooo, everybody," Carrie sing-songed. "I hope you have room for two more special Santa decorations." She waved to Miles. "Let's set them near the front of Santa's sleigh."

Miles gave Jo a helpless shrug and followed Carrie to the front of the sleigh. She placed her box on the floor and carefully lifted the lid before motioning for Miles to hand her the second box.

"Attention, everyone." Carrie clapped her hands. "I'm sure you're all anxious to find out what surprise I've been working on for this very special event."

Delta eased in next to Jo. "Have you seen it yet?" she whispered.

"No," Jo whispered back. "I..."

"Shh..." Carrie held a finger to her lips and frowned at Jo and Delta.

"Sorry," Jo apologized. "Carry on, Carrie."

"Thank you. Now, as I was saying, when I found out Jo and all of you were hosting Santa's workshop, I said to myself, 'Carrie Ford, surely there is something special you can contribute.' I started looking around, and it's as if the Good Lord himself showed me what to do."

"What is it?" Santa Gary craned his neck, trying to catch a glimpse of the contents.

"Without further ado, let me introduce Sparkle and Twinkle." Carrie reached into the boxes and removed two identical figurines. "Santa's special elves."

There was a moment of shocked silence. Jo's jaw dropped as she stared at the grotesque leathery faces. Tufts of gray hair jutted out from the edge of the green and red striped hats.

The "elves" were adorned in black velvet jackets. One of the elves grasped a wooden toy train while the other held a small sailboat in his leathery hand.

A thick layer of white fur-lined the matching black pants. Shiny red shoes completed the ensemble.

Delta said the first thing that popped into her head. "They're gremlins."

"I..." Jo squinted her eyes and studied the faces. "What exactly are they?"

"Well..." Carrie carefully set them on the cement. "They're spare parts from some of my other projects."

"What kinds of parts?" Jo asked. "Never mind. Maybe I don't want to know."

Sherry clamped a hand across her mouth. "What is that smell?"

"They smell?" Carrie sniffed a gremlin's hat. "I don't smell anything."

"I smell it too." Kelli curled her lip as she waved a hand across her face.

Carrie's face crumpled, and Jo thought she was going to burst into tears.

"You probably can't smell them since you're around the preserving liquids all of the time." Jo motioned to Nash. "I think we should set them near the door to give them a chance to air out a bit."

"But the kids won't see them," Carrie whined.

"I hope not," Delta muttered. "It'll give them nightmares."

Jo gave her a warning look. "Actually, the front is a much better spot. That way, the children will see them on the way in." She carefully picked up the gremlin and carried him to the doorway. "I would hate to see them get knocked over. Perhaps if we set them right here." She set the gremlin near the side service door.

Nash, who had picked up the gremlin's twin, placed it next to Jo's.

"See?" Jo wiped her hands on her slacks. "This is the perfect spot. Everyone can admire them before anything else."

Slightly placated, Carrie grudgingly nodded. "Yes. I think the children will notice Sparkle and Twinkle."

"Of course, they will." Jo gently guided Carrie back inside. "I'm sure Delta can use some help with the refreshments."

She did one last check to make sure the gifts were in order, and the tables filled with hot chocolate, apple cider and the trays of Christmas cookies were ready to go. Along with the presents, Jo had assembled small gift bags for each of the children.

The sound of tires on the gravel drive caught Jo's attention, and she ran to the doorway. "They're here."

Nash flipped the switch, illuminating Santa's workshop, his sleigh and the reindeer. Twinkling Christmas lights blinked merrily along the back wall, above the overflowing piles of Christmas gifts.

Excited chatter filled the evening air as the children scrambled off the bus.

"Ho. Ho. Ho." Santa hopped onto his sleigh, giving the beard one more quick scratch. "Who do we have here?"

With Pastor Murphy's assistance, the first child hesitantly approached the sleigh.

Santa leaned forward, eyeing the small child through his wire-rimmed glasses as he read the nametag on his shirt. "Braedon Greer." He motioned for him to come closer as the pastor nudged him along. "I heard you've been a very good boy this year."

Braedon nodded, his eyes round as saucers.

Santa consulted his "nice" list. "Santa has a special gift for you."

Sherry, Santa's elf, darted to the pile of presents. She grabbed one and quickly returned, handing the brightly wrapped package to the child.

"Th-thank you."

Santa placed a gloved finger on the side of his nose and winked. "Now be a good boy and Santa will see you again next year."

Mrs. Claus guided the boy to the table, where Jo was waiting to hand out the goody bags. She bent down to eye level. "This is for you."

Braedon reached for the bag. "Are you from the North Pole too?"

"No," Jo solemnly shook her head, "but I am a very good friend of Santa and Mrs. Claus."

"You're lucky." He inspected the paper bag covered with smiling snowmen. "Can I open this?"

"Of course." Jo's throat started to clog. "The gift is for Christmas Day, but you can have the goody bag now. I'll hold your present."

The boy hesitated, reluctant to release his grip on his special gift from Santa.

"I'll give it right back," she promised.

The boy nodded before handing it to her. He tore off the sticker before reaching inside and pulling out a coloring book and crayons. Next, was a candy cane, a chocolate marshmallow snowman and a popcorn ball. A set of racecars and a pair of warm mittens were at the bottom of the bag.

He carefully placed the items back inside the bag before reaching for his gift.

"We have hot chocolate and cookies over here." Jo led him to the table where Claire, Marlee and Carrie stood waiting to serve their guests.

Jo returned to the table that was filled with goodie bags and greeted the next child.

The gift giving and cookie consuming passed by in a blur. Santa finished visiting with the final child. Moments later, as if on cue, the sound of music echoed into Santa's workshop.

Marlee hurried to the doorway. "They're here."

"Perfect." Jo clapped her hands to get everyone's attention. "We have one more surprise." She motioned for them to follow her out of Santa's workshop and to the Nativity Nash had secretly been working on for her.

It was the best gift she could've ever imagined, and out of everything he'd made, the manger scene was her favorite.

The Christmas Star was centered above the manger, and Mary, Joseph, Baby Jesus and the wise men were beneath the star. Instead of sheep, Jo had improvised with her faithful pup, Duke.

Even Curtis had managed to make an appearance and was swatting at a pile of straw beneath Jesus's cradle.

The church carolers gathered next to the Nativity, waiting for Pastor Murphy's signal.

For a magical moment, there was silence. Jo lifted her gaze to the clear night skies, the stars twinkling brightly above. She sucked in a breath and started to sing, "O Holy Night..."

The end.

If you enjoyed reading "Divine Christmas," would you please take a moment to leave a review? It would mean so much to me. Thank you! - Hope Callaghan

The series continues...Divine Cozy Mystery Series Book 6 Coming Soon!

Books in This Series

Divine Cozy Mystery Series

After relocating to the tiny town of Divine, Kansas, strange and mysterious things begin to happen to businesswoman, Jo Pepperdine and those around her.

Get New Releases & More

Get New Releases, Giveaways & Discounted eBooks When You Subscribe To My Free Cozy Mysteries Newsletter!

hopecallaghan.com/newsletter

Hope Callaghan Books

Samantha Rite Mystery Series

Heartbroken after her recent divorce, a single mother is persuaded to book a cruise and soon finds herself caught in the middle of a deadly adventure. Will she make it out alive?

Waves of Deception: Book 1
Winds of Deception: Book 2
Tides of Deception: Book 3
Samantha Rite Box Set – (Books 1-3-The Complete Series)

Garden Girls Cozy Mystery Series

A lonely widower finds new purpose for her life when she and her senior friends help solve a murder in their small Midwestern town.

Who Murdered Mr. Malone? Book 1
Grandkids Gone Wild: Book 2
Smoky Mountain Mystery: Book 3
Death by Dumplings: Book 4
Eye Spy: Book 5
Magnolia Mansion Mysteries: Book 6
Missing Milt: Book 7
Bully in the 'Burbs: Book 8
Fall Girl: Book 9
Home for the Holidays: Book 10
Sun, Sand, and Suspects: Book 11

Made in Savannah Cozy Mystery Series

A mother and daughter try to escape their family's NY mob ties by making a fresh start in Savannah, GA but they soon realize you can run but you can't hide from the past.

The Family Affair: Book 9
Pirates in Peril: Book 10
Matrimony & Mayhem: Book 11
Swiped in Savannah: Book 12
Turmoil in Savannah: Book 13
Book 14: Coming Soon!
Made in Savannah Box Set I (Books 1-3)
Made in Savannah Box Set II (Books 4-6)

Cruise Ship Cozy Mystery Series

A recently divorced senior lands her dream job as Assistant Cruise Director onboard a mega passenger cruise ship and soon discovers she's got a knack for solving murders.

Starboard Secrets: Book 1
Portside Peril: Book 2
Lethal Lobster: Book 3
Deadly Deception: Book 4
Vanishing Vacationers: Book 5
Cruise Control: Book 6
Killer Karaoke: Book 7
Suite Revenge: Book 8
Cruisin' for a Bruisin': Book 9
High Seas Heist: Book 10
Family, Friends and Foes: Book 11
Murder on Main: Book 12
Fatal Flirtation: Book 13
Deadly Delivery: Book 14
Reindeer & Robberies: Book 15
Transatlantic Tragedy: Book 16

Southampton Stalker: Book 17
Book 18: Coming Soon!
Cruise Ship Cozy Mysteries Box Set I (Books 1-3)
Cruise Ship Cozy Mysteries Box Set II (Books 4-6)
Cruise Ship Cozy Mysteries Box Set III (Books 7-9)
Cruise Ship Cozy Mysteries Box Set IV (Books 10-12)

Divine Cozy Mystery Series

After relocating to the tiny town of Divine, Kansas, strange and mysterious things begin to happen to businesswoman, Jo Pepperdine and those around her.

Divine Intervention: Book 1
Divine Secrets: Book 2
Divine Blindside Book 3
Divine Decisions Book 4
Divine Christmas: Book 5
Divine Cozy Mystery Book 6 (Coming Soon!)

Sweet Southern Sleuths Short Stories Series

Twin sisters with completely opposite personalities become amateur sleuths when a dead body is discovered in their recently inherited home in Misery, Mississippi.

Teepees and Trailer Parks: Book 1
Bag of Bones: Book 2
Southern Stalker: Book 3
Two Settle the Score: Book 4
Killer Road Trip: Book 5
Pups in Peril: Book 6
Dying To Get Married-In: Book 7
Deadly Drive-In: Book 8
Secrets of a Stranger: Book 9
Library Lockdown: Book 10
Vandals & Vigilantes: Book 11
Fatal Frolic: Book 12
Sweet Southern Sleuths Box Set I: (Books 1-4)
Sweet Southern Sleuths Box Set: II: (Books 5-8)
Sweet Southern Sleuths Box Set III: (Books 9-12)
Sweet Southern Sleuths 12 Book Box Set (Entire Series)

Cozy Mystery Collections

Cozy Mysteries Collection (Heart and Holiday Edition)
Cozy Mysteries 12 Book Box Set: (Garden Girls & Cruise Ship Cozy Mystery Series)

Fall Into Murder 6 Book Fall Themed Cozy Mystery Collection

Audiobooks
(On Sale Now or FREE with Audible Trial)

Key to Savannah: Book 1
Road to Savannah: Book 2
Justice in Savannah: Book 3

Cozy Mysteries Cookbook

(Free eBook version w/Newsletter signup)

(Available in Paperback to purchase)

Cozy Mysteries Cookbook-Recipes from Hope Callaghan Books

Meet Author Hope Callaghan

Hope loves to connect with her readers! Connect with her today!

Never miss another book deal! Text the word Books to 33222

Visit **hopecallaghan.com/newsletter** for special offers, free books, and soon-to-be-released books!

**Facebook: facebook.com/authorhopecallaghan/
Amazon:amazon.com/HopeCallaghan/
Pinterest:pinterest.com/cozymysteriesauthor/**

Hope Callaghan is an American author who loves to write clean fiction books, especially Christian Mystery and Cozy Mystery books. She has written more than 70 mystery books (and counting) in six series.

In March 2017, Hope won a Mom's Choice Award for her book, "Key to Savannah," Book 1 in the Made in Savannah Cozy Mystery Series.

Born and raised in a small town in West Michigan, she now lives in Florida with her husband. She is the proud mother of 3 wonderful children.

When she's not doing the thing she loves best - writing books - she enjoys cooking, traveling and reading books.

Delta's Divine Granola Recipe

Ingredients:

4 cups rolled oats

3/4 cup wheat germ

3/4 cups peanuts

1/2 cup roasted pumpkin seeds (or pepitas)

1/2 cup finely chopped almonds

1/2 cup finely chopped pecans

1/2 cup finely chopped walnuts

1 cup unsweetened shredded coconut

3/4 teaspoons salt

1/4 cup brown sugar

1/8 cup maple syrup

6 tablespoons cup honey

1/2 cup coconut oil

1/2 tablespoon ground cinnamon

1/2 tablespoon vanilla extract

Directions:

-Preheat the oven to 300 degrees F (165 degrees C). Line two large baking sheets with parchment paper or aluminum foil.

-In a large bowl, combine the oats, wheat germ, peanuts, pumpkin seeds, almonds, pecans, walnuts and shredded coconut.

-In a medium saucepan, blend salt, brown sugar, maple syrup, honey, coconut oil, cinnamon, and vanilla.

-Bring to a boil over medium heat.

-Pour heated liquid over the dry ingredients. Stir thoroughly.

-After stirring, spread the mixture evenly over both baking sheets.

-Bake in the preheated oven until crispy and toasted, about 25 minutes, stir once halfway through.

-Let cool completely before storing in an airtight container.

*Makes ten cups or approximately 2 lbs.

Great for gift-giving.

Made in the USA
Las Vegas, NV
05 July 2023

74261860R00215